MURDO

An Anomalous Rite

H. Z. Khorion

ISBN: 099940380X
ISBN 13: 9780999403808

TABLE OF CONTENTS

CHAPTER 1
THE RENEWAL

Beyond the window of solitude, a night passed away. The calling was back. Discretely, I closed the door and descended the wooden staircase carefully avoiding the planks I knew would squeak.

Gliding along the Persian rug, I quietly crossed a parlor of subdued light and shadowy ghosts of antique furniture. Drawn by the serene pull of dawn's delicate light wafting in through the vestibule's stained glass, it felt as if I were merging into a new reality. Then the thrilling sprites of a new sun appeared and beamed in an ecstatic energy that invited the soul to a novel frontier. I was about to open the door.

"So, Willie! What will you be doing for vacation?" asked an abrupt voice of gossipy inquisition.

"Almost made it," I said to myself, twisting down the end of my mustache.

I hadn't seen the landlady standing there in the adjacent coat room. I couldn't really object to her question. It's just that in those moments of serious contemplation, I need the luxury of unperturbed quietude so often presented by day's earliest hours. I knew she couldn't have understood.

The old girl had on her blue dress and matching vest. Curls of blued hair contrasted against chandelier earrings and a necklace of pearls. The smell of talcum powder affirmed her readiness for church later in the morning. She looked good for her age, but I was surprised by how early she was up. I knew she meant only an amiable greeting, but this question would have been so less painful later in the day. I hadn't even had my first cup of coffee.

"I haven't decided as yet, Mrs. Franklin." I calmly said, buttoning up my leather jacket."I'll let you know as soon as I know."

Stepping out of the old brick house at the edge of Boma, I caught the distant beat of a rumbling train and the earnest voice of a determined engine. The syncopated clatter of a hundred wheels sounded a theme of dedicated certitude pounding on beyond the fleeing darkness of yesterday's night. Briskly I headed out into the cool dawn.

I wished I could find my own certitude. I needed to think. Walking along the road to town, silhouettes of distant forests slowly gave way to the brilliant arrival of Helios, god of the sun. Due drops gleamed in the grass.

Early birds chattered in important meetings scattered amongst the tops of sleepy trees and the tired wires of human twaddle. I began to wonder if Mrs. Franklin had had time to fill her bird-feeder.

"Maybe that's why she got up so early," I thought.

Refueling airplanes of businessmen, sportsman, and rouges was the only job I'd ever really liked. In spite of the chronic restlessness of mind, the solitude of the vast grounds at the airfield, and the curious intrigue of transient characters always lured me back for another day. It was the only job where I'd lasted long enough to earn a vacation. The next two weeks were all mine.

Crossing the bridge at Sundog River, the churning mystery of flowing time brought to mind the many good friends that had passed away in years gone by.

"Good friends, that's all that really matters," I thought, hands gripping behind my back."I miss them. At this stage of life, I can't expect many more vacations. I have to make this one count. I have to think."

Yet, beyond the goals of conscious reason, an insistent calling kept stirring at the fringe like the subtle swirls in the waters below. Crossing the river, a cacophony of crows suddenly erupted from somewhere beyond an old factory building. There they used to make propeller hubs, but now frayed wires and forgotten pipes cast long shadows that crept along the retired walls of glowing bricks and heroic graffiti.

It had been a mild winter for Ohio. Now in late February, early shoots were already breaking ground. Buttercups, bluebells, and chickweed all swirled in random parties, waving and reaching in an Orphic ballet that splashed across the pathway. I tried to step over them, but almost tripped over the matted vines of seasons gone by. So many possibilities. I thought I might get lost in the jungle of competing thoughts.

"God…. Any suggestions?" I said, looking up to heaven.

Early sunbeams painted impressionistic scenes of gold and purple clouds morphing and scattering throughout the vastness of an infinite space. Just then a beacon appeared! A bluish beam drifted across the sky, pointing the way to courageous fans exhausting the greasy signature of the town's oldest cafe.

Arriving at the café, I strolled on back through the busy atmosphere of perking coffee and frying bacon. The Sunday morning convention was well underway. Themes and insights sailed across the U-shaped counter like snow flurries in competing winds. It seemed Fate had reserved for me the last seat at the end of the counter. Familiar faces and unconscious nods authorized my attendance.

Taking my place on the worn out stool, my arms eased in along the familiar rills of counter top maple polished by the sleeves of countless connoisseurs and volunteer experts. For the town folk regulars, Boma Street Cafe was an extension of their own kitchen, complete with gossip and ongoing news analysis. I never knew what new insights might emerge from the morphing themes that animated the back counter symposium.

The ambient murmur of background voices and legato clinks of lazy teaspoons, created a psychic cushion that rested a worried mind.

"Coffee," I said, as my favorite waitress cruised by in her red skirt and checkered apron. "And try to make it a recent vintage."

Terse glints from savvy eyes started my day with the energetic spice of a cavalier rebuke.

"Now then … maybe I can really concentrate on how best to use this vacation time," I said to myself.

As I sat trying to think, I couldn't help being distracted by an emerging crescendo of strident voices assailing the usual atmosphere of congeniality. Dangerous plans with grave consequence displaced the vapid prattle that normally occupied the Sunday morning coffee club.

Vocalizations became increasingly urgent; their proposals increasingly radical. I tried to glean a validity in the specious arguments sliding around the counter-top like salt shakers at rush hour. What I was hearing was a shocking neglect of individual judgment that betrayed the gravity of the topic at hand. I didn't know the rules of public conversation, but the emerging consensus seemed irrational, dogmatic, and dangerous. I was astonished by the ease unchallenged presumptions could morph into certain convictions.

"Group-think is not serious analysis," I thought to myself. "Maybe if I question the group's cherished premise they might consider rational discourse about a critical issue."

"If the leader is presumed always right, then what's the role of the individual's thoughts?" I said to the group.

From the disapproving stares of the burger joint regulars, one would have thought I had just violated their most sacred tradition. Maybe being myself was too assuming.

"Just who do you think you are to question the president?" said an old veteran as he snapped open yesterday's newspaper.

Proud metals clinked with staccato emphasis. He seemed hurt, indignant, and angry. The subject of discussion had nothing to do with who I am. But I could see that there was no point in saying anything more.

I just sat there gazing into the old clay coffee cup. I tried to count the fading strata of yearly coffee rings, just wondering what treasures a microscopic expedition might discover. In the cafe ambiance, I could feel the shallow anger of disapproval morphing into smug dismissal. Then the topic of the round table switched to yesterday's basketball game.

"Nothing wrong with basketball," I thought. "But bombing a foreign country demands a little more justification than the narcissistic hyperbole extruding from a patently corrupt president."

But that kind of conversation was simply off the table. The leader is always right.

"Either we fight 'em over there, or we fight 'em over here. So bomb them!" the old veteran had said.

Long ago I used to think like that. But what could I say now?

"Don't they value the judgments of their own selves?" I wondered.

In my younger days, the concept of "my own self" had been an object of serious philosophic inquiry. Nowadays I was just happy for a day off from work. As breakfast faded to lunch, the cast of characters rotated anew like waves of geese flowing in seasonal migrations.

Just then the gentle jingle of the antique doorbell provoked a glance to the front of the café. A Cajun roustabout I had met a few times before stopped in for the chili-lunch special. He was a short, stout man with a beard of stubble and a countenance of innocence.

"Hey, Jerome," I said.

I could see in his eyes something serious was on his mind. He was headed my way. I listened sympathetically as he exhausted his misery and frustrations involving an entanglement with a certain gal of his. This was to be a three-cup story.

On the counter top of life, humble gestures of work-scarred hands and sorrowful squints of wistful eyes played out a drama of betrayal and struggle. Yet, a kindness in his bearing shone clear and true. I was proud of his spiritual strength. I knew he would survive the crisis. It seems his adventure had been an Easter egg hunt in a briar patch, but I found more interesting the humanity of his character than the particulars of his saga.

His story left me exhausted. I took a long pause of empty thought, just sitting and mindlessly staring in the coffee cup, my reflection at the bottom. Then I felt a strange impulse. Its intentions obscure, its energy autonomous. Jerome was finishing off his chili when suddenly I surprised myself with a spontaneous utterance:

"Jerome!" I said."... What is the meaning of 'self'?"

He looked at me, then turned and looked down to the soul of the bowl. I wondered why I had even asked. He was very quiet. Then, in that curious aura of a Cajun séance, Jerome carefully stirred and conjured and slowly nudged the chili pepper entrails like an oracle divining for ancestral wisdom. His cowboy boots shuffled and scuffed along the checker board flooring, encoding yet another glyph amongst the cryptic signatures of countless shoes that chronicled the stories and tragedies that informed the history of his species.

Jerome looked up and out the big window beyond the counter. His ears turned and tuned as if to sense a distant call. Discreetly, from my pocket, I eased out a small note pad and pencil.

Then, in a quiet voice that spoke more to himself than to me, he said, "All it takes is one little squirt."

Insights gleaned from time in the pen reminded me some enigmas were best left alone. I turned away for a moment and then looked out the big window hoping to catch a glimpse of this phantom of truth. Just then waitress looked up from a bottle of ketchup.

"Hey, maybe you should be paying rent coming in here like this," she said.

I left the café to walk the rainy streets of introspection. Morning clarity had given way to afternoon's overcast. Intermittent rain and drizzle glazed the streets of an enduring town. I chose to walk the long way back. The extra distance would be an andante meditation and perhaps an invitation for inspiration. The walk along the neighborhood lanes of simple homes smelling like cabbage eventually lead back to the old factory building I had seen earlier in the day. The detour brought a new perspective.

I could no longer find that provocative graffiti: "know thy self". It was there this morning carved in the starkness of February's sunrise.

"Where did it go?" I wondered.

Brooding clouds of afternoon sky had cast a darkness over the whole countryside, completely changing the mood of the old factory. A railway spur of rusty iron lead the way through overgrown fields. Wild flowers camped out in family clusters, just waiting to wave at engineers that never come.

Leaning posts of rusting fences limped along in abandoned trails of soggy weeds that once formed a well-groomed yard. Distant echoes of working men lingered on in abandoned workshops of a ghostly factory. An old chair of weather-mauled wood sat leaning against the remains of a brick stoop.

"...Who all sits there...?" asked the whistling voices of swaying pines.

Stealthy shadows roamed the vacant windows of an epoch long gone by. Its obscure secrets rescued by the climbing vines of an underworld empire. It was starting to rain again.

Approaching Sundog River, the steady applause of thrashing currents cheered on the resonant echoes of impromptu melodies bubbling up from zealous currents haunting the stoic archways and limestone pillars of a bridge lost in time. Beneath the chilly beams of tenured girders, brushstrokes of shivering waves appeared and disappeared through mysterious clouds of swirling mist.

The wet grayness of superstructure steel gradually merged with the gray aloofness of searching fog. Like magic, the surreal union of steel and mist induced a vision of an alternate world. On a vanishing bridge, I lost sight of both ends. Then I was walking on fog! I grabbed the railing and stepped on with care. Intermittent rain and wind buffeted clothes now smelling more like doughnuts than avgas.

"Just who do you think you are?" kept echoing through my mind.

"Who do they think I am? And why would that matter?" I said to myself.

I sloshed on past the bridge as the chilly drizzle soaked my socks and wilted my cap. But early flora reached up and rejoiced in the gift of steady rain.

"Indeed, who am I?" I said.

Long ago, an artist friend had raised this very question. We used to spend all day in his barn discussing arts and metaphysics. The concept of an authentic "self" was a frequent topic. Ivan had said it was the source of creativity. I never quite understood that. The idea of finding my own "self essence" seemed tantalizing yet confoundingly elusive. The question lingered on for years even after he moved away. Alone, I kept seeking.

A philosophy student once told me, "You don't have a 'real self.' You're a bundle of traits. 'Self' is a delusion fabricated by the machinery of mind for administrative convenience."

"So what is this subjective - experience - of - being thing that's been asking ?" I wondered.

Then there was the military. They had said : "you're a name, rank, and serial number."

I had to ask myself, "So what could be this corporal's 'self' that questions them?"

But it was the local shoe salesman, he had the answer all along.

"Yessiree, blue suede shoes," he would say."That's definitely you."

I'd been through a lot of shoes since those days. The labors of subsistence tended to displace the metaphysical inquires of youthful leisure. Paying the rent was now the central endeavor of life. Yet, at the fringe of mind, a lingering question fermented in secret. Random bubbles conspired as I went.

Walking on to the rooming house, I tried to think, " 'Self'? Perhaps Jerome is right. A squirt? ... Maybe I should ask that phantom of truth beyond the big window."

Then I happened to look up. A willow tree along the bank began swaying in the wind and rain. It was waving to me. Above and beyond the willow, a crow ascended upwards, climbing up through mist and turbulent clouds. That crow. It reminded me of one of Ivan's paintings I had seen long ago. I watched him the day he painted it.

". . .comes with the wind, goes with the rain. . ." he would say.

I knew that meant something vital.

"I surely wished I'd asked him at the time," I thought."But that was a long time ago, and now he lives far, far away in Oregon."

Somewhere in the distance a church bell sounded. Another step, another step, then . . .

"Oh!" I said with epiphanic glee.

I hurried home to pack for an overdue journey.

CHAPTER 2
AN OVERDUE TRIP

Next morning, I retrieved a duffle bag from under my bunk. This turned out to be an archaeological dig that strained the limits of allergic tolerance. But the dusty excavation turned out to be the easy part.

"I never seem to get this right, taking things I don't need, needing things I don't take. Sure am glad for the opportunity to visit Ivan again. Maybe now I can find an answer," I said to myself. "Better take a notebook just in case."

"We're just passing through," I thought."At our age, this is probably the last chance for a visit. I'll bet he's got that same old guitar. I'll take my recorder."

Later that day, I called Ivan's house to invite myself over and asked for directions. His woman answered with surprise.

In that mellowed out voice of her folk singer persona she said, "... He told me to tell you he was lost at sea ..."

For a moment I was concerned, but then I realized she meant the sea of dreams.

"The old trickster still has it," I said to myself.

The aging Ford had endured many projects. Duct tape, rusty dents, and leaking oil were all the proud badges of noble campaigns of years ago. But it wasn't over. Next morning, I checked out the vehicle. Baggage, tires, oil, gas, all okay. With the brave willingness of an adventurous old codger, the truck finally got started, ready for a new expedition.

Morning sun had mostly melted the spotty islands of nomadic frost squatting across the windshield. Rolling steam from the coffee thermos curled up and condensed on the windows sketching out little crosses of rime.

"I'll be a long way from home," I said to myself as the truck warmed up. "I should plot with care the route of the trek and log with discipline the mileage and fuel and money expended. What will Ivan be like after forty years? How can I ask a man so sensitive for the answer to life's most brutal question?"

One more sip. I was headed West. Whistling joints and fluttering tape provided company through morning's early light. Traffic was sparse.

"I've never been headed this far west. Glad I brought extra oil," I thought.

Crossing the border to Indiana brought a distinct change in mood. It was a feeling of homey serenity in contrast with Ohio's formal deadlines. The ground seemed greener. Pastoral farms and proud homes with Pickett fences lead the way to small villages of cottage industries and local enterprise. Railway crewmen milled around a station built with brick and pride.

"What adventures await them?" I wondered.

An idling locomotive gazed out at morning's glistening tracks. Its obscure ambitions rumbling in code. Creosote spiced the atmosphere.

Transiting further into the grain states, the rustic scenery of Midwestern tradition, gave way to the monotony of mono-culture regimentation. Flat terrain invited miles and miles of agribusiness. Its monotonous themes of devastated wildness enforced an ethos of atrophied imagination. Boredom was becoming painful. The dullness seemed like a slow motion lobotomy. I wanted to dream, but I couldn't.

Ahead on a state road west, distant glints signaled the approach of oncoming traffic. Brilliant reflections of morning sun flickered and flashed in random peeks.

"Something's coming... What is that?" I thought."It's too small to be a truck or car. Maybe a motorcycle ... No, it's too wide. The thing has a shimmy, probably needs an alignment whatever it is."

Then I heard the sound of helicopters: "...Chop, chop, chop,... chop,... chop, chop. . ."

Zoom! Just then, a dune buggy streaked past me in the opposite lane. The signature clatter of the Volkswagen voice reminded me of a time long ago when I first met Ivan.

CHAPTER 3
ARTS AND CRAFTS

It had been a morning of frustrating indecision. I had finished high school the previous June. By winter, dozens of brochures from obscure trade schools and military recruitment fliers had piled up like a pyre ready to consume the body. My parents had said I was supposed to make good career choices if I ever wanted to be a good citizen, but the choices seemed so overwhelming it was making my head hurt. I sat out on the porch trying to think. It was the last day of winter. I was searching for something.

An arts and craft show was in progress in downtown Boma. The distant atmosphere of burning hot dogs and competing themes of folk band melodies compelled an accelerated walk to the center of town. The street had been blocked off all around the courthouse. Hundreds of voices blended together in a burbling zoo of human cacophony. The major key of the phatic festivity signified a mood of gaiety.

Artists and craftsmen from around the county had come to display their wares and promote their industry. Pottery, baskets, jewelry, leather, and custom-made auto tags. All strewn along Main Street in a sedentary parade of booths, tents, and pickup trucks. Crowds of people strolled around inspecting the originality of the crafts on display, each one an expert. All full of free advice. Cars and trucks kept streaming in, searching for a niche to set up their booth. It reminded me of the midway at a fair.

A noisy buggy caught my attention. The boisterous clatter of its patched-up muffler sounded like a percussive ensemble of helicopters. If it had ever been a traditional car, it was now customized beyond the limits of acceptability.

"This is not normal," I said to myself.

It was a show just watching this guy set up. I had to walk over. Tubes of steel formed the body; oil dripped from the rear engine, and the plywood nose cone had become a fold-out table with drawers of tools and handmade jewelry. The roof of patched-up canvas looked like a quilt of salvaged remnants.

He was a lanky guy in raggedy pants and a leatherjacket that blended in with a necklace of teeth and metal amulets. Long black hair bore the tangles of deep thought. The curled-up fringes of his burned-out beard stood out like a secondhand wire brush.

"This guy is weird. I'll have to check him out," I said to myself.

"Sir, is this vehicle street legal?" I asked.

He just sat there on a crate tinkering with his guitar, strumming a Latin beat to the steps of an ant trekking across the table. It was as if he hadn't heard me. Then he reached into a bucket of amulets and pulled out a smooth river stone. Rotating it around, he carefully inspected it as if it were some kind of ancient scroll.

In a slow and deliberate voice, he said, "...You don't have to be criminal to be an outlaw... , but for some people it might help... "

Chaotic arrays of brass and silver and polished stones lay diffused in patterns of handmade curios. I held one up to the sky. Intricate detail of a Japanese Maple shone through the quarter size slug of stainless steel. Canvas flapped in the breeze.

Looking into his vehicle, I couldn't help noticing a wooden crate on the passenger floor. Happenstance winds fluttered pages of paintings revealing canyons of clouds and fish with human faces. Fir trees with pointy hats sheltered bikers and naked women. One painting depicted a museum of tree stumps. I wondered if this guy was a mental case.

"It'll grow back," he said, pulling on the remnants of his beard.

He reached into a spittoon wired to the floorboards and pulled out a handful of rings, pendants, and necklaces. He laid them out in random patterns across a card table. With closed eyes, he slowly waved his hand over the works. Suddenly he reached down. A shiny piece, he picked it up and studied it with grave intensity.

Then in a cautious voice he said, "... This is what you need."

The oval pendant of sterling silver was about size of an almond. A lone crow stood on a fence post looking out over the horizon. Delicate incisions depicted in great detail the feathers and claws and eyes. Even the intricate grain of the wooden post shone clear in its silver medium.

"This is what I need?" I said.

Noon's glare glittered across the array of metal curios.

"What precision," I said, turning the piece over and over. "This must have been milled under a microscope. What do you get for these things?"

"Who knows," he said as he took a sip from the little brown bag stowed under the seat. "... Comes with the wind, goes with the rain ..."

"You can't make a living unless you specify a price," I said.

He refused my dollar.

"Who is this guy?" I wondered.

I looked the piece over again, then noticed the tiny engraving on the back. "Ivan."

"Never heard of him," I said to myself.

Ivan was dressed like a hobo and smelled like kerosene. His face bore the scars of after-hour knife fights, his guitar no less a veteran. His voice revealed a contempt for the conventional and a leaning to rebellion. He seemed so deviant. I began to think he might be subversive. Probably a communist. But he was certainly talented.

"How is this done?" I said, looking over the pendant.

Looking dismayed, he sat on a bucket and took a labored breath of disgust. His eyes wandered out across the lanes of human zoology grazing the corrals of asphalt. He looked on past the court house and store fronts that lined the streets of consumer pretense. Then gazed up and over the veneer of modernity tacked to the arching bricks of a forgotten epoch of craftsmanship. His eyes beamed up to the sky, flying on beyond the distant towers floating in haze. Finally, his expedition came to a stop on the roof of a nearby temple. He winked at the gargoyle as he laid his hands on a disk of brass around his neck.

"... It just tunes in like a distant station," he said with the quiet voice of a dejected priest.

I was wondering if I had just been insulted. Perplexed, I spent several minuets looking over his works trying to grasp his meaning. But just then, the smell of popcorn drifted in from a nearby booth.

"Oh ... is that like when you remember a dream you thought you'd lost for good?" I said.

Ivan blinked. Then he reached down to adjust a buckle on his boot. Foreign words consulted the teeth of his necklace. Then he pulled out a knife and began peeling an acorn.

"Come on over," he said as he leaned back and propped up his feet.

"Now why should I go and visit a Bohemian subversive?" I thought to myself. "I'm sure he's counter cultural. Yet his work is so intricate and its themes so amazing. This guy is crazy, but just for fun, maybe sometime I'll go and visit his shop. That should be interesting."

Later that spring, just out of curiosity, I road my bicycle just beyond the city to the address on his card. I found a stone house covered with vines. It looked almost like a natural rock outcrop. The house was dark, moss covered the stone steps. I was beginning to wonder if it had been abandoned.

"Where's Ivan?" I wondered.

Then I noticed fresh tire tracks. Following the tracks a few tens of yards, I could see Ivan's dune buggy behind the barn. An oil lamp shone through the encrusted window. Hardwood smoke rolled over the stove pipe chimney. Then a large black dog trotted up the dirt path barking authoritatively. I moved slowly as he walked me to the barn. I think he was part Labrador.

The faint scent of stale hay and vintage manure wafted by the rusting gates of an overgrown pasture. The barn was a grand figure, its sun-ripened timbers aged to the hue of bib overalls. Tufts of weeds poked out the warped siding like ear-hairs from somebody's grandpa. It reminded me of an old farmer I once saw at the feed store.

As I approached the door, the precarious roof of rusting steel provoked a measured apprehension. A chorus of squeaks and clicks from somewhere above accompanied the passage of noon day's clouds. The knob and tube wiring didn't inspire any confidence. For some dumb reason, I was expecting an organized shop. I stepped in.

Along the dirt floor, work benches clustered in family coveys: a drill press, a grinder, and an old dentist drill with tiny bits. Brushes and pastels and vials of strange liquids populated the dining room table. Looking in a stall, I noticed an easel set up on a mattress. Rifles relaxed in every corner.

"How does this make any sense?" I wondered.

The barn was part machine shop, part arts studio, and part living quarters. A wood stove stood in center. Native artifacts and witch doctor fetishes lined one wall. Original paintings and engravings lined another. A possum hide stretched across a post. The barn smelled like burnt sausage.

"Ivan, about the pendent you gave me at the craft show," I said.

He was seated on the dirt floor with a reloading press bolted to a board lying across his lap. I sat down to watch. Then he picked up the bullet he had just reloaded.

"Forty-one magnum," he said. "Lots of potential. You never know its destiny until it happens . . . like being yourself."

"Ivan, about that pendant at the fair. It was so fine, how was it produced?" I said.

"Oh . . . ho. . . .'Curiosity!' I guess you could start there. Creation is as broad as the sky and as elusive as yourself," he said.

"Creation?" I said."I meant what was the technique of its manufacture?"

Ivan reached behind an acetylene tank and pulled out a board. It was a crude and colorful impressionistic painting of a simple woman dressed in burlap sitting in a garden, her hands reaching forward to a bucket of wet clay.

"What is this?" I said.

"Oh, that's Woman. She's about to sculpt Dozer. I painted it with chop sticks," he said with pride.

Slowly and carefully I looked all around in the picture.

"So . . . where's the Dozer?" I said.

Ivan winced and waved his hands as if sculpting an imaginary figure in midair.

"About!" he said sternly." 'About' It isn't here. It's going to be, maybe. 'About' is always going to be, maybe. And only the guides know where dogs go. Maybe he'll show up in your dreams if you ever find yourself."

After a pause of consternation, I said, "So . . . whatever does my 'self' have to do with this? Look, I have my ID right here in my wallet."

Ivan got up and walked to a series of shelves nailed between barn polls. They were stacked with paintings and sketches and sculptures of clay. He reached for something. The first painting was a primitive pioneer man. His face of weary creases matched the tattered cracks of his leather jacket. Jagged scars told the stories of wilderness survival and weather's brutal moods, death and sorrow, triumph and humility.

"It takes endurance to find it," he said.

I looked in his face for a hint; I looked in the painting for a clue.

"Find what?" I said.

The next painting was a green and yellow frog just staring into a pond. It had an expression of great satisfaction about something.

"What's this one about?" I wondered."Perhaps the smoking revolver in the background might be a clue. Maybe I shouldn't ask."

Ivan looked over and said, "Yeahaaa…and sometimes it takes radical introspection."

Then another painting. The precarious view from a mountaintop ledge induced an uneasy vertigo. Morning sun painted the infinite space of distant clouds scattered above charging rivers and treacherous mountains populated with thousands of sentient fir trees with long green beards. Their tops pointed like crude hats on village elders. Whole clans swayed in family meetings. Birds swept through in wavy formations. Bison and rabbits grazed the ground. Bees and wild flowers reached out from the foreground. I studied it for several minutes. Ivan had put tremendous work into this.

"It's a whole new world once you find it," he said in the faux voice of a gravelly pioneer.

The glint in his eye acknowledged my appreciation of his work. It was almost as if he were inviting me to try.

"I wonder if I could do something like this," I thought to myself. "But where would I start?"

"Creation doesn't come with directions," he said sarcastically, "but the Carp people... now they always paint by the numbers. They never leave the cave, and they don't remember their dreams. But creativity . . . it's you yourself, your own path. There's no maps beyond the frontier. Not for any of us. Being alive is living on the ledge."

We sat on the floor next to an oil stove sipping Chinese tea. A block of oily wood on a car jack served as a table. Ivan pulled off his boots and tinkered with a guitar.

"There's Tree people, and then there's Carp people," he said, strumming a minor chord. "The Trees ... Their arms reach high to the upper world, their roots reach low to the underworld. They feel the winds of heaven and the magic of dreams, the moods of Earth and the spirits of the deep. They're always creating the unpredictable, always seeking the unknowable. They are their own selves."

"And then there's the Carps," Ivan said, strumming a major chord. "Carp people live in shallow waters driving in circles, eager to consume the crumbs of banality, happy to be the lie of the day and proud to wear the badge that proves it. They always play in four forty square notes."

Ivan handed me a piece of cardboard and a stub of charcoal. An oil stove, a tea pot, and a pair of old motorcycle boots sat before me.

"I'll bet you can do it," he said. "Just create what you don't know."

I sat there staring at the cardboard, then looked all around the barn.

"What am I supposed to do, Ivan, how is it done?" I said with subdued timidity.

"They put one over on you, didn't they?" he said, his jocular voice barely masking a subtle grimace.

Just then, Dozer walked into the barn and lay down with a catch between his paws. He was chewing on a piece of fabric, slobbering all over it, tearing it and ruining it. It looked as though it might have once been a veil . . . maybe.

"Here, Dozer, let me see," Ivan said.

He took the remains and held them up to his eyes and looked all around the world.

"Fantastic!" he said turning to me, "Hey, amigo, ... if Dozer can see through the veil ... "

He handed me the chewed up remains, then reached for a mason jar.

"This is disgusting," I said.

I threw the frothy mess to the floor. By accident, it hit the cardboard forming chaotic patterns of splats.

"Farrrr . . . Out! Now there's a good one," he said.

"I didn't do this," I said, pointing toward Dozer.

Ivan got up and said, "You'd be surprised. . ."

Ivan pulled over an old shortwave radio from behind a box of chains. It was missing the cabinet. It looked as though he'd made certain modifications. We sat on the dirt floor as he tuned around the band. I could hear lots of buzzes and static and occasional stations. Then Ivan found his favorite station: Radio Havana. They were playing that polyrhythmic beat only Latin salsa can make. But the signal would fade in and out. I leaned toward the radio trying to hear.

"Static's typical for this time of day," he said as he adjusted the home brew antenna tuner. "Just listen, feel its beat, embrace its soul, imagine you're playing along with them."

"I play recorder, not guitar," I said apologetically.

"... Well then here! ... Just play trombone," he said as his hands rose up and began sculpting in midair the syncopated harmonies of Latin voices. "Look, Dozer's playing base strings."

The station faded in and out as Ivan adjusted the radio. For a moment the static became worse, but then the cowbells brought it back.

"Static is nothing," he said. "Just listen to that piano racing up and down the keys chasing the trumpet. The congas will take you right through. Cha Cha Cha. Just get in the groove."

Then he began playing along with the vibraphones. I listened in amazement.

"Vibraphone. . . . What a beautiful sound," I thought. "Its golden notes floating like angels..."

I was getting into this. Then he handed me a flute.

"Now come in on the beat," he said as he motioned to the vocalists.

"Just get in the groove," I thought.

Ivan adjusted the antenna. The static had faded away. I was surprised at the joy of playing along with the happy mamba of a distant station from somewhere across the Caribbean. Its rhythm irresistible. My foot began tapping the ammo box.

Ivan looked over to Dozer and started to grin. I was amazed to discover I could hear right through the static. Even Dozer was wagging his tail to the Latin beat. Then Ivan emitted a ghoulish snicker.

I was still playing marimba when I said, "What's that?"

It emitted a whistling, whipping sound. Around and around, Ivan whirled the cord like a sling shot. Its voice came in right on the beat. I thought it was some kind of native musical instrument. It wasn't.

"Hey! ... That's the antenna! You can't do that!" I said in protest. "I was just … You disconnected the antenna. I've just been playing along with static!"

I felt like a fool.

"You tricked me," I said in defensive embarrassment.

Ivan walked over to Dozer and said, "Look, his foot's still tapping."

"You disconnected the antenna . . ." I said with a prosecutor's arrogance.

"But ... for a moment you connected yours ... " he said in quiet reserve.

Ivan sat down getting comfortable leaning back against an old '39 Plymouth. He said it had been his father's car.

"Father was an anthropologist until the day he died. Still have his pipe," he said. "Handmade gift from Patagonia."

Ivan poured us another cup of tea using a travel trunk for a table.

"So what will you be doing after high school?" he said.

I was still looking over the old radio, wondering what he had done to it.

"Courage can help too," he said, trimming his fingernails with wire cutters.

"I plan to join the army," I said with patriotic pride.

Ivan flashed a grin as he leaned toward the open barn door. Daisies waved in the gentle breeze. Woman went about planting tomatoes.

"Farrr out!! I'll bet that'll be interesting. 'Yes, sir. No, sir.'...How about: 'Maybe, sir' ?" he said, leaning back against the old car.

"Well, you can't have an army unless you have obedience," I said authoritatively.

Just then, Dozer walked over and sat on the cardboard of veil scraps.

"So, so, so. . . .Is obedience marching in step with a phony myth? Or tapping your foot to a distant salsa?" he said with a vague sarcasm.

"What does that mean?" I said.

"Get off the grid," he said, reaching into his cigar box.

Ivan got up and put the pistol in his belt. Stealthily, he infiltrated himself over to a dark corner of the barn. It seemed to have once been a horse stall. Narrow sun rays streamed in through cracks in the warped siding. A roughhewn post glowed with the jagged stripes of a jungle canopy. He stopped as if to sense a distant call. His cautious hesitation was making me nervous. Then he checked the cylinder of his six gun. "Click." I stood up and cautiously walked over. The stall was locked with a huge bolt through a hasp. It took two wrenches to unfasten it. Then he slowly opened the stall door.

"What's in there Ivan? Why is it locked?" I asked with an apprehensive voice.

Old hay scattered along the ground. A native mask hung on a nail, and an unhinged attic door leaned against the post.

"This is nothing," I said with a relieved voice.

Ivan sat on the ground and carefully picked up the old attic door.

"Have a seat," he said. "Once you find it, you'll never be the same."

I couldn't imagine what he was talking about. I sat in the hay thinking this had to be a game. Maybe it was a checker board. Spider webs hung like theatrical curtains. The antique latch had been broken outward as if kicked out from inside the attic. The hinges were bent. Then I noticed the teeth marks. An uneasy feeling stirred my guts as he slowly turned around the little door.

A blurred jumble of flying colors induced a feeling of falling through an exotic jungle. Gruesome scenes of war zones floated by in cubes of ether. Structures of impossible geometry confused my point of view uncontrollably. Caged figures of distorted creatures provoked a pathetic depression like being at a midway freak show. I wanted to look but felt guilty of something. At the center of the work, a coiling storm of foaming stars dissolved right through the board. Its accelerating whirl stretched out terrified nudes. The lines and weaves of graphic ambiguity kept shifting and jittering as though the work were moving. Monstrous tentacles began reaching out.

"Is that you?" he said quietly.

"Ivan! What is this Thing-painting? This is totally immoral. I don't want to see it anymore," I said in disgust."Did you do this?"

"... And sometimes it takes a surreal shock," he said getting up.

I didn't know what to say. It was as if he were in a different world. I got up and followed Ivan to the garden.

"Amazing, these herbs," he said."Your own aesthetic is half the reality."

Woman was busy planting spring produce, white half-runner beans, potatoes, onion, peppers, tomatoes.

"We belong to Earth, it's not Earth that belongs to us," she said, waving to the garden.

Then I was confounded by the sight of a peculiar mass of welded steel.

"Ivan, whatever is this?" I said with a surprised voice.

I looked the work over with puzzlement. I guessed it had been a tricycle, but three diesel horns and a steel jib sail were welded to the handle bars, a bear trap formed the jaws, and a steel box loaded with fool's gold replaced the seat. Tattered remains of welded chains formed a curled tail.

"Trisauracycletops," he said. "Wild imagination can ride you there if you let it."

"How's that?" I said.

"Just look up at those neutrino storms, you can guide them with your spirit you know," he said, looking on past the scattering clouds.

Bees buzzed the wildflowers growing up through the spokes below.

"Look up. It's not what you look at that matters, it's what you see," he said, quoting Thoreau. "... comes with the wind, goes with the rain. . ."

For a moment, I had a sudden awareness of being.

Then he laid down in the garden and said, "Here, help me make that cloud disappear. Static is everything."

The visit wasn't what I'd expected. The world seemed more mysterious than ever.

"I better get home now, Ivan. I'd like to come back sometime," I said.

Riding home, I struggled to make sense of this bizarre visit.

"What's the big idea with that Thing-painting?" I wondered. "And the radio static? What was I hearing? What does this have to do with who I am?"

I hurried home to experiment with my own shortwave. I was up most of the night.

Scheming rays announced the arrival of summer's morning. It was my day off from the hardware store and I decided to take a walk. But as I stepped off the porch of my parent's house, a pigeon bombed my hair. I wiped my head with a hanky and looked up in anger, ready to cuss the bird. Roaming clouds of intrigue and morphing moods of aloofness ridiculed the insidious atmosphere of convention. Then an unexpected breeze fluffed my hair and reminded me of a disgusting experience.

"That Thing-painting I had seen last spring at Ivan's place, why would he ask if it were me? Don't I already have a 'self'?" I thought.

It was as if my identification were a hoax. Just thinking about it provoked an anger like being insulted. It was scary. I never wanted to see that Thing-painting again.

"Not that I'm too afraid," I thought. "Surely any art critic could revoke its legitimacy. Whatever was Ivan thinking to construct such a thing? Or did he even do it? I'll bet it's still there."

Just for exercise, I walked the mile to the Bohemian's barn. When I entered, I found Ivan barefoot and hunched over an ammo-box illuminated by a single light bulb suspended from the rafters above. The dust of antique hay slowly rolled through the air, highlighting the sunbeams streaking in through gaps of weathered siding. Cats played in the loft. Dozer guarded the door mat. He looked up, wagged his tail, then went back to sleep. I started looking around for that Thing-painting. Ivan didn't look up or emit any greeting, but I knew he was aware of my presence.

His attention was intensely focused through a headband magnifier onto a single drop of red wine precariously stationed on a small square of prepared ivory. Then a scalpel appeared from under his palm like a magician withdrawing a card from the fourth dimension. Skillful hands began to slice ever so slowly into the drop of wine.

"Whatever are you doing, Ivan?" I said.

After a metaphysical pause, a low voice that invoked a feeling of grave crisis said, "Seeking the essence."

"Essence? You can't find an essence like that," I said with a presumptuous naiveté.

Ivan continued slicing at the now diffusing spirit. Each slice cutting little groves in the ivory, liberating the essence of wine. Bizarre incisions and alien silhouettes began to emerge. But then he just stopped. I drew closer to this scrimshaw of chaos. We both looked down at the work. On the ivory was a small patch of crisscross incisions filled with the remains of a wine drop. It was about the size of a postage stamp.

"Hey," I said, "maybe this could be modern art for leprechauns."

Ivan rose up, eyes burning red. His face contorted like a carnival show horror monster. Suddenly, he lunged at me with the scalpel! I jumped back and tripped backwards to the ground. Then a blast of insane laughter ignited the atmosphere.

"Farrrr Out!" he said."For a moment I could feel the essence, but she got away."

Then he picked up his guitar and flopped down on a pile of old tires.

"Ohhh. . . . I once knew an essence, her name was Constance, she brought joyance and grievance to many a peasants, she put out all she could along her grooves of red, then vanished in a puff of fragrance. Ohhh. . ."

"Who's Constance?" I said.

"Your self is what you are the moment of creating what you don't know. It's always a surprise. ...Comes with the wind, goes with the rain. . ." he said, wistfully looking out the window as ghostly veils of hypocrisy fluttered like curtains at the end of time.

In a pause of quiet introspection, I began to wonder if I would need a scalpel to find my own essence.

Ivan looked over directly to me and said, "So, so, so, amigo...yes, no, maybe!"

I knew I would have to return.

It was a chilly afternoon in a quiet town and a restless yearning filled my shoes. I stepped outside and inhaled. The earthy aroma of autumn's spirit charged my head with life's mysterious awe.

"Amazing," I thought."Every day is absolutely unique."

Liberated leaves swirled in flocks, each one seeking out its own path. Each one striving for that underground station to new adventures. Each one queuing up in excited expectation, just waiting to board the train of eternal seasons.

It reminded me of a poem Sister Helen once read in my high school class. It likened the leaves of autumn with the death of old friends. A nearby crow called to another. Just then I remembered last night's dream. It was about Ivan. He was reaching out through a canvas to touch its meaning. I thought it really strange. It had been several weeks since our last visit.

"Wonder what he's up to today?" I thought.

As I approached the barn of the Bohemian, I though it odd the front and back doors were standing open. As I entered, a chilly emptiness invoked a pathos of being lost. Embers in the stove glowed in meditative calmness. Ivan's chair was vacant. Dozer's mat curled and flapped in the breeze. I stepped out the back door. Nothing. I stood there at the edge of a neglected pasture, wondering…

But then a distant voice of an earnest beat stirred my spirit. The steady meter of its compelling chant provoked a strange attraction to the wilderness.

"Bong, bong, bong, bong."It had the tempo of an urgent jog.

Something was calling me. I turned my head side-to-side, searching for its bearing. I set off in search of the source. But the barn's growing shadow concealed a treachery of stabbing thorns and malicious thickets. This was an ambush in waiting. I looked all around. There was absolutely no clear path toward the sound.

There it was again, "Bong, bong, bong, bong."

I would have to make my own path through the field of entanglements. I wished I'd brought a machete. Sloshing along through tall grass and mean thistles, I stepped awkwardly over tree limbs and scattered rocks. A vine caught my foot and flipped me into the briers. Pulling off stickers and burrs, I tromped on, listening and searching for the source of this magical voice. I began to think maybe I should have been looking for natural pathways. A deer path, a rabbit path, any creature's path would do. Sometimes they led the way, sometimes not.

Stopping occasionally, I listened again, refining my bearings to the source. Over insulting weeds and insidious clumps of rusting iron, my footsteps became higher and longer. Then, "THUD!"

"Damn!" I said.

The hard drop jarred my bones and sprained by ankle. Climbing out the sink hole, I found my knees engraved by the scalpels of geology and my tongue mashed by the teeth of carelessness. This journey was becoming dangerous, and I was becoming exhausted. But something was calling. I tripped again and fell in a ball of barbed wire. By now, scrapes and cuts covered my arms and legs. Rips and tears ventilated bloodied clothing. A dog barked in the distance.

"Maybe I better turn back while there's still daylight," I said to myself.

But as I got up, the transcendent aroma of burning herbs inspired a step beyond. I followed the limping shadow that reached ahead. A gate was open. Autumn's quilt of fallen leaves hugged the earth with themes of joy. Browns and maroons lead the way, and a carpet of moss embraced a bolder. Walking became easy.

Just then I spotted Ivan in a clearing along a tree-line next to the river bank. He was squatting on his haunches between the dune buggy and a log. He seemed to be working with something. I approached carefully. A bowl of a reddish tea sat on a rock next to the smoldering remains of a campfire. Fumes of vinegar and dung hung heavy in the air. They were making me dizzy. A crescent wrench rested against an oak tree. Roots reached out across the earth, twisting and arching into little caverns of darkness. He was humming something.

I couldn't imagine what he was doing. He was holding up a large machine bolt while blowing smoke through a log. It was the same bolt he had shown me last summer. The one he had found along the railroad tracks long ago. He said it had called him.

"Bong, bong, bong, bong."There it was again, loud and definite, the resonate sound of a rail bolt striking cadence on a hollowed-out log. Waves of modulating smoke carried the beat to the upper world.

I sat on the ground, watching, listening, sensing. I was trying to understand this. A drop of blood slowly diffused through the little veins of a fallen leaf. The rhythm was mesmerizing. Then he abruptly stopped.

Slowly looking up, he said: " ... 'Yourself' ... it's your own path."

His unblinking eyes scanned the woods in urgent expectation. A foreign snap from somewhere near provoked a suspicion of something lurking. I looked about.

Afternoon sun rays filtered in through stoic branches of conspiring trees. Long shadows of secret pathways sneaked along the fields of tangled weeds. Ivan's eyes swept on through the forest and beyond the remains of a stone fence. Then his gaze slowly merged with the flowing ripples of a chilly river and sailed along its murky trail until the voyage disappeared under the mossy curtains of an abandoned bridge. As dusk hushed over us, he lit a kerosene lantern. In silence, he stared in the lamp for a long pause of meditation.

Then, as if I were a lunatic's apprentice, Ivan said, "Here, help me invoke the ghost of this stubborn poet. He's been here before, I could hear him, but he wouldn't come out."

"Ivan's beginning to get really weird," I thought.

He grasped the bolt by the head and pressed it to the earth, pushing and twisting until it finally augured into the ground. Then he carefully turned it with the crescent wrench. Adjusting it like a piano tuner, he tweaked the bolt a little at a time. One way, then another way, then just a tad more. Suddenly, he jerked back as if shocked by a high voltage resonance. He dropped the wrench and cupped his hands over the bolt. Then he blew into it as if it were a little campfire.

"Feel it?" he said.

Briskly, Ivan rubbed his hands together until a tingling sensation bloomed between them. He encouraged me to follow along, to try. I knew I had to try this. Briskly, I rubbed my hands together as Ivan hummed a cryptic invocation. I began to feel the tingle.

"Orpheus," he said in a special voice tuned to the tone of Hades.

Trembling, his tingle-filled hands hovered above the bolt, absorbing the spirit of the underworld. Something jerked his hands, pulling them up and around and around, and then plunging them down into that bowl of mysterious tea. The lantern began to flicker.

The shadowy ascent of dripping hands shimmied as if captured in a spell of the supernatural. He jerked again as unseen forces pulled his hands up to the twirling heavens, then slammed them down to an old tree stump. Splat! He took a heavy breath as he slowly raised his oozing hands and revealed a smoldering image. I gasped as I witnessed a ghostly figure of an unknown character smoking up and arising right through the stump.

"Ivan! What is that?" I said in disbelief. "Can this be real?"

But then the figure dissolved into a cloud of smoke and floated away into the darkness of a knowing forest.

"... Comes with the wind, goes with the rain ..." Ivan said to himself.

He looked over toward me with that furtive grin of his. Staring with the gaze of a possessed shaman, he groomed his beard with the consecrated residue of an anointed ghost. For a moment, I could feel it. But then I lost it when I realized this was impossible. At times, Ivan could be spooky.

"I've got to come back," I said, as Ivan rode me home in his old dune buggy.

For weeks, I thought about this peculiar journey.

It was toward the end of winter that the scene of scattering clouds in a morning sky brought to mind one of Ivan's paintings.

"What a thrill it would be to paint a scene like this," I thought."Ivan said creativity might take a surreal shock."

I set off on the brisk walk to Ivan's place and found the country road colder than expected. Crows lined the phone wires. Cows huddled along the fence line. On reaching Ivan's road, blue smoke of a hardwood fire promised a welcome radiance from the stove inside. As I approached the barn, I could smell the evocative musk of linseed oil. I thought he must be painting. I jogged ahead, eager to see what he is doing.

He was painting all right. But when I entered the scene, I had to abruptly stop. The model was his woman. She was totally unashamed wearing only a small veil over her eyes. A thin veil. Nodding, her hair waved like a willow tree in the wind. She was waving to me. I took a tentative step toward the canvas. I wasn't quite sure what to do in this situation.

Steadily focused on the canvas, Ivan said, "Hey, hey, hey, amigo. Seeing through the veil, that's how you find yourself."

I looked up at the model, then looked over at the canvas.

"Seeing through the veil. . . ?" I wondered.

On the canvas, above and beyond the figure, a crow was ascending upwards, climbing on through mist and turbulent clouds. Crow was wearing only tinted glasses that seemed to be riding sunbeams infiltrating down between kingdoms of mountainous clouds. I looked over at Ivan not knowing what to say.

He paused a moment, then in the subdued voice of a retired professor, said, "I never know what I'm painting until it happens."

Just then Ivan scooted a whisky jar across the jewelry bench. Sparkling reflections flashed my eyes as the illicit brew caught the glittering beams of sunlight streaking in. Wobbling palettes of liberated rainbows staggered across the bench and climbed the hands of creativity. Then a golden talisman stirred in the sunbeams, mixing them together with the vital themes of egg yolks pouring out from an antique inkwell. Ivan's hand held the brush as it received the sacrament.

His eyes narrowed and reached out to the aura of a distant world. Crow glanced back in a jest of psychic resonance. Eye to eye, the magic brew of golden sunbeams guided the brush on its mystical journey. A critical tension filled the air. The eyes of Crow began to glow. The magic space of creation was about to open. Suddenly . . . Contact! Eyes of Crow dazzled like sunbeams. Ivan jerked back from the canvas. Grinning like his drunken dog, he raised up the magic jar and took a careless pull.

"Kaw, Kaw, Kaw," he said to Crow, wheezing between words, "Now . . . our worlds are connected."

Still focused on the canvas, Ivan passed the jar over to me.

In the somber voice of a pirate about to be hanged, he said, "The essence amigo. . . .Comes with the wind, goes with the rain . . . You have only to look up."

A torque swept through my stomach as I realized I was about to confront an awkward dilemma. I looked in the jar. I thought the world of Ivan, but I really didn't know if I could handle this. Little balls of hydraulic oil and clods of renegade blood rolled along the bottom, stirring up bits of solder and flakes of gold. Horse hair filaments and streaks of paint and dead gnats all swirled around like lost souls in a prehistoric river.

"Play what you don't know," he said turning to me.

"I just don't know about this," I thought to myself looking skeptically in the jar.

I looked up. My mind went out the window, over the tree tops, past the clouds, and beyond the horizon of winter's last day. Baffled by the crux of the quandary, I boldly inhaled a breath of faith.

"Whoa! ...Wow Wee!" I said.

A juju of volcanic fumes shot up my nose and enlightened my ears. Eyes began watering with dazzling streams of solar flares. Kurt vapors of seething spirits cast a spell that invoked the gods of adventure.

". . .Ooooh, I think I feel it," I said as my mind went completely blank.

"Viva la Revolucion!" I said as I took a hardy pull from this elixir of transcendence.

I've never been quite the same ever since that day. That evening, Ivan had driven me home in his father's old Plymouth. It was drivable though it had been an ongoing restoration project. Riding along, I felt the nostalgic spirit of a forgotten era. I wondered what all it had been through.

A few months later, Ivan called. He had moved on to Oregon. The sense of loss stabbed my soul. That was forty years ago.

CHAPTER 4
THE PLAINS

Suddenly, traffic became heavy. Lanes of cars converged like the squeezing hairs of a ponytail. Herds of trucks stampeded in like the rambunctious roundup of thunderous bulls. "Better pay attention," I thought. I was now approaching the Mississippi Bridge. Somewhere ahead, in a looming dusk that signaled the end of an epoch, a reunion awaited. I had to wonder how well Ivan had aged over all the years. I should have stayed better in touch.

I drove on, propelled by the thought of witnessing a river that had inspired writers, musicians, and artists. Who knows, maybe the ghost of an unknown poet lurked there, just waiting to commune through the veil. Crossing the Mississippi reminded me how far I had come and how far I had to go.

"Will I ever find myself-essence before I die?" I wondered as dusk faded to night.

Davenport Hotel afforded a view of sparkling reflections as distant street lights roamed the quiet waves of introspection. I tried to sleep. But a presence stirred at the fringe.

Back on the road, the flatness of the terrain, though not unexpected, was strikingly unfamiliar to Midwestern eyes. Driving the straight roads of a flat state became utterly boring. Agro monopolies had whole counties under till. Clouds of bugs roamed the sky. I was looking forward to passing Iowa.

In the vastness of the plains, distant storms cruised the horizon. One was fast approaching. It was coming directly toward me! I pulled over to the side of the road. The voice of prudence urged flight to the opposite direction. The voice of adventure urged embracing the unknown.

First came a sudden gust of a powerful wind. Trees bowed and waved in excited anticipation. Thrashing leaves cheered and whistled, taunting the gods before the main event.

"It's Thunder Head Zeus versus Titan the Terriblllle!" announced the gods of competition.

The sky turned yellow then dark purple. Cool winds howled as rippling muscles of rolling clouds clashed in a spectacular struggle for the heavens. Lightning bolts let fly all around, then crashed in terrifying flashes. Distant thunder got the last word. Stratified watercolors streaked across the closing curtains of a calm drizzle.

"That was quick," I said to myself ."And to think, every storm is different."

The next morning, I left Mom and Pop Hotel at Elk Point, South Dakota. I had called Ivan from the lobby to let him know the progress of the trip.

"Should make Gillette by nightfall," I said, looking over the map.

He said, "Go north to Sioux Falls, then turn left."

That sounded simple enough. It was. But these plain states, they were much longer than I expected, and gas stations were becoming increasingly sparse. I monitored the fuel gauge as it went from full to near empty. I was sure glad to see the next road sign.

"Gas: Next Station 50 Miles," it said.

I thought it wise to gas up while I had the chance. Driving up the crumbling driveway, I came upon a dilapidated station. The sign hadn't exactly lied; the station was here alright. But it looked as though it had been closed for the last fifty years. The stop might as well have been an archaeological expedition, but it had its own aesthetic aura.

A nostalgic ambiance of hydraulic oil seeped up from the fading ruins of Paleolithic asphalt, its embedded bottle caps now collector items. Pealing stucco from leaning walls hung precariously over old phone lines now connected only to the ether. A garage door was wide open, just waiting for the next phantom customer. Out back slumped an old truck. Its crazed windows sprouted tree limbs like a post-retirement hobby. Its door ajar as if to invite the ghosts of an era long gone by for one more joyride. I could almost hear them. The kids. They used to hang out here.

Fuel and water were becoming scarce. I had to proceed on this trek with increasing care and budget limited resources with increasing discipline. I was running low on fuel. I never knew when I might see that "Next Gas Station 50 Miles" sign again. There in the plains of South Dakota, I stopped at the next town that seemed to be inhabited.

CHAPTER 5
A STRANGE DETOUR

Murdo was a nondescript town of mundane character along the endless road westward. I stood there filling the old Ford with gas. Chilly winds buffeted my ears and stung my feet. My eyes began to water. Then my attention wandered over toward the truck window.

"There, right there, that's my stuff from Ohio and the totality of my life's meaning. That's me," I thought, looking in the cab. "And now I'm standing here in the plains of South Dakota a thousand miles from home. All I have for security is this old truck. And it's got the mileage of a trip to the moon and back."

A feeling of insular vulnerability crept over my being.

"What did early explorers feel visiting this region for the first time?" I wondered.

My focus drifted to my own reflection in the window. It looked like some wandering stranger looking in.

"Who is that guy?" I wondered. "I'm a long way from the security of home. Am I really doing this? Does this make any sense?"

It was as if the festering question of "self-essence" was trying to escape from the subliminal prison of conventional worldview and assert itself as an independent agent, fed up with the banality and security of what passes as the acceptable life.

"Well, this is the whole point, isn't it?" I thought.

I paid the fuel bill and started to leave the station, but then I noticed a sign across the road: "Car Show." I thought I'd probably never pass through here again.

"A quick tour of a novel show could only broaden the mind," I thought.

Outside a humble barn, the sign said, "Car Show," but inside it looked more like a world class car museum.

"In this little town? Sure glad I stopped in," I said to myself.

There were hundreds of old classic cars, all lined up in barns and garages, all expertly restored to showroom finish. I thought it odd such an amazing place could be so devoid of tourists. It seemed I was the only customer.

"If this is a 'show,' then the performers must be spirits from a time long past," I thought. "All these old cars. What stories could they tell? I'll bet that old Linotype machine knows."

I took an abbreviated tour that found a Tucker, a Studebaker, a 1957 Chevy Bellaire, and even a Pierce Arrow, with certain modifications. The restored vintage gas station evoked memories of the old days back in Boma. Just beyond the jukebox, Elvis Presley's own Harley Davidson motorcycle stood provocatively parked amongst the icons of his day. An excited corn husk doll peeked out from the curio shop window.

Another section held pioneer antiques, archaeological artifacts, local minerals and the petrified remains of prehistoric flora and fauna. I had to take a quick tour. This was utterly fascinating .

Stationed along the walls were old west slot machines, antique firearms, and an old time fiddle. Player piano in the corner was just waiting for pay day festivities. Then the creaking floor lead the way to display cases of arrow heads, fossilized fish and ammonites. ... all these prehistoric fossils... What were the hopes and dreams of these creatures of so long ago? What would be left of me in a million years, I wondered. Then, looking intensely through the glass case, completely absorbed in a fossilized Ginkgo leaf, I began to feel it… that rare feeling when one is being intensely watched. Just a creepy feeling, probably my imagination. But then it grew and grew. Suddenly, I felt an irrational alarm of danger. Primitive instincts compelled my immediate attention. "

"Confront this predator NOW!" I said.

Immediately I turned about. Right there, right in front of me, right before my eyes I met face to face the mounted head of a stuffed moose.

"Let's see, if I leave now, I can make Gillette by evening," I thought.

Driving westward through town toward the highway entrance ramp, I kept thinking about that staring sensation.

"Some people call it a psychological delusion," I thought. "But still, it seemed so real. A stuffed moose?"

Almost at the end of town, I spied a small café. A good cup of java would be just the thing. A mediocre joint, stranded along an interstate road, transiting the land of coyotes, squatting on a plundered continent, enduring the presumptions of an entitled population, adrift somewhere in some possible universe. I went in.

Something seemed unnatural. I was the only customer. And my truck, it was the only vehicle in the parking lot. I had not met anyone along the road through town. Looking around the establishment, I though it odd the place could be so empty of patrons this time of day. I requested coffee. The waitress seemed aloof and preoccupied. Not quite rude, just remote.

I began thinking about the time, years ago when I was a kid. Daddy had taken me to a fine restaurant for lunch. It was one of those dining rooms that had real silverware on a real linen table cloth. He let me sample the coffee. It was a wonderful tang, an eye opener, a communion with the gods. Been spoiled ever since. Then the waitress brought a cup. I'm not sure what it was, but I noted that this was a joint with plastic utensils and a vinyl table cover. I sipped it the best I could. It might be fifty miles to the next café.

I looked around again, looking both ways, confirming the vacancy of seats and booths that should have been alive with the ongoing stream of highway customers.

"Vacant as a haunted house," I thought.

Alone in the café, alone at a table, just me alone hugging this cup of industrial discharge, that's when that creepy sensation of being watched was upon me again. I didn't like this set up. I thought it best to leave now. I got up and paid the bill. About to leave, I was just hoping the waitress would ask me "How was everything?" I had a ready answer locked and loaded. But she never asked.

"This stuff is so rancid, they'll need a Hazmat team just to clean the coffee pot," I said to myself. "But I guess it's not really her fault."

Stepping out of the café, I was stunned by how beautiful was this clear day. I looked up and took a deep breath and thanked God for air. As I walked to the truck, I noticed a crow on the nose of the hood. It was kind of funny. It looked like an over-sized hood ornament just watching me. But then he took off heading west. I thought he must be on his own journey.

"Good luck, Crow," I said, waving to my fellow traveler.

Getting in the truck, I checked the maps, reviewed the route, and got ready to roll. It was three o'clock in the afternoon. But something odd was happening. There, in front of the truck, there appeared two flat, circular, fuzzy lights suspended in air. It was as if the head lights were on and reflecting from an invisible wall, but I checked and the headlights were off. And there was no wall, and even if there were a wall, headlight reflections would not be visible in the daylight.

I backed away from the lights. As I did, they too bounced and backed away synchronously with the truck movement. As I turned while backing up, the asymptotic motion of the lights mapped out, in pantomime, an invisible wall. I evaded this first wall. A second pantomime wall appeared across the parking lot. Hard maneuvering evaded this phantom too.

"Sure glad to get away from those walls," I said to myself.

Uncharacteristic apathy dulled any urge to investigate this extraordinary phenomenon. The absence of any curiosity concerning these anomalous lights was rather negligent of a supposedly intelligent being. I kind of knew that, but it didn't seem to matter. Something was wrong. I couldn't imagine what, and that didn't matter either. My only thought was to return to the highway and continue the journey. For what purpose? I had no idea. A novel phenomenon was at hand, and I'm just ignoring it.

"Well, that's because this is silly," I said.

Heading out to the access road, a confusion descended upon my head and provoked a feeling of apprehension. I just knew this was going to be fun. An invisible force intruded on the steering, guiding the truck onto the main road. I didn't care.

The highway began to glow the color of gold. The sky was starkly clear above the sparse lands of a South Dakota afternoon. All except for one cloud with a silver lining hovering above just ahead of the truck. It was profoundly beautiful. It was as if I were floating on clouds of warm feathers.

"GOD NO!" I yelled in panic.

Horrified, a weightless vertigo knotted my stomach. Baggage, maps, and canteen all floating by in a chaos of dust and confusion. Ears burning with unbearable pain. An incredibly loud roaring, howling, screaming whistle filled the truck.

Just then pilot instincts kicked in: I reached for the dash to close the throttle.

"Stop the spin with the rudder! Raise the nose! C'mon baby, we can salvage this," I said.

I looked for someplace flat, any place flat. Nothing. I looked for a horizon. Nothing.

"Damn, this is a truck!" I said.

I expected to see very soon, a rushing ground sweeping by as the truck was likely tumbling in this final of all final approaches. But there was no ground. Nowhere at all.

"Never give up," I thought.

As the seconds screeched by, I was surprised by the emergence of a fatalistic acceptance of death and by the peace of mind and calmness that now enveloped my psyche. This was new territory. It was this novel tranquility that enabled a focused assessment of the scene outside the window.

I was surrounded in all directions by a dull, silvery overcast sky that seemed miles away, leaving a clear but ambiguous space in the immediate proximity. A shiny dashed line, like a highway center line but brighter, appeared ahead. It was an absolutely straight dashed line that vanished into infinity. But there was no road. The dashed line was just suspended on air rushing under the truck at highway speed.

Overlaid on the distal overcast was a network of stratified clouds, miles away and light in hue. They stretched out like strands of taffy forming irregular ribbons of horizontal and vertical bands that interlocked in lumpy knots to form a closed grid all around.

Ahead, there appeared a narrow archway extending up from the truck's nose to about twenty feet above where it then looped back down, its legs separated by the width of the truck of about six feet. It looked like a giant hair pin with the base almost touching the front of the truck, but displaced forward about a foot.

This was certainly a peculiar archway. It glowed like a neon lamp, bright red against the silvery sky. It wiggled like a bowl of glowing red Jell-O transiting over railroad tracks. This glowing, wiggling, red archway would, from time to time, split, forming two archways yet joined at its base. Slowly weaving back and forth, the two archways would split then reunite, split then reunite, all the while wiggling, all the while howling, all the while speeding down this road of absurdity, propelled by forces incomprehensible.

Beautiful little dew drops slowly trekked across the windshield. Pearls of light cautiously pacing in deliberate starts and stops, carefully contemplating their next move. One after another, they were living beings armed with faith and love, exploring and seeking their own calling while bravely facing an unknown frontier. What courage.

Suddenly I awoke with all the clarity of a new year's hangover. The gravity was back on. The noise had stopped, the truck had stopped, the engine had stopped. I too was stopped. I was just stopped, just sitting there, confused, trying to make sense of anything. I looked about, the cab was a mess.

"What's going on?" I wondered.

Through the window, I perceived the ambiance of a thin fog illuminated by diffuse lighting that had no particular source. It was like being at the park on a misty overcast day. I cracked open the door. I could see that the truck was parked on a broad, gray surface. It looked like a pad of wet granite. As the fog began to lift, I looked up and ahead. About twenty feet in front of the truck there stood a wall.

This wall seemed to be made of polished granite with shiny specks of mineral scattered throughout. There were no visible seams in the wall. It looked to be a monolithic structure. It was about twenty feet in height, and its width extended indefinitely to the right and left to vanishing points beyond the horizon.

"This isn't looking like any ordinary truck crash," I thought."I don't know if I'm dead or alive. But this place…it doesn't look like any orthodox vision of heaven or hell. Maybe I made it to Purgatory."

As the fog lifted, I looked about. Then I saw them. I don't know what they were or how they got there, but they were definitely different. Three of them stood there by the wall, one to my left, two to my right. I just knew they were watching me. They reflected no light at all; they were shadows but in three dimensions. Each figure, revealed in the topography of what seemed to be long over-sized robes, was approximately anthropomorphic having a head, body, and limbs; they stood five or six feet tall. No reflective feature could be seen, yet I immediately perceived from these sentient umbra the telepathic constructs that functioned as communication. In their shadowiness, they "radiated" a psychic presence that announced their character as intelligent beings.

Having made peace with death, I had already transcended the fear of the unknown. I didn't fear these things, whatever they were. But the anger of being shanghaied on this impromptu detour demanded an explanation. I suspected that they, these shadow beings, were responsible. But perhaps not.

"Maybe we're both captives of the same mysterious phenomenon. But what could that possibly be?" I wondered.

I didn't want to insult them with false accusations, but I wanted to know. And a good questioning is not an accusation. I decided to exit the truck, close the door, walk right up to them, and ask them who they were and what they were doing, but being careful only to ask of them what I would be willing to answer about myself. I wanted to get to the bottom of this without breaking anything.

I introduced myself and then asked them their names. It felt really weird standing there trying to speak to three dimensional shadows. They were very quiet. To look at where a face would be if they had one, was to look into an abyss. It was like staring into one's own eyes in a mirror on a moonless night with the lights out.

"I know a presence is there, but I can't see it," I thought to myself.

The three of them just stood there, staring into me with an invisible gaze of unfathomable depth.

Spells of dizziness rolled through my head like waves slapping a rocky shore. And I staring into them, felt a profound solitude of liquid space that flowed to eternity.

Suddenly, a psychic radiance emanated from the leader. A force infiltrated my brain and formed a complete circuit between the other and myself. I could feel this bilateral loop swirling through my head, involuntarily shuffling through by mind, auditing ideas, syntax, and vocabularies. A novel mode of communication began to emerge.

"Bent Triangle," he said, introducing himself and then his two associates, "1-2-3, and Point".

His helpers nodded a hesitant greeting as from one with marginal communication skills. I nodded back to reassure them the success of their tentative communication. Besides his name, I had a lot of other questions for this Bent Triangle guy.

Without any hesitation, BT answered everything, easily and completely. I knew everything about him and his whole project. I felt a complete relief. But the content of this question-answer session quickly evaporated like the theme of a dream after a good night's sleep. I did not care if I forgot the questions or the answers. Though I carried a small note pad and pencil in my pocket, my mind was so dull I couldn't think to take notes. Then something about that wall attracted my attention.

At some point during this meeting, the question of my entrance into their "castle" came up. I didn't know if he asked me, or if I asked him, or if somehow both at once. But I definitely indicated that I wanted to go in and explore.

Bent Triangle said, "Do you know what you're saying? Do you know what you mean by asking to enter?"

For a moment, I glanced down at the pad and questioned my sanity. I wondered if his helpers could understand what was going on.

"Certainly, I want to go in and see inside," I said looking up.

I looked left and right along the wall with utter amazement. This thing has no beginning, no ending.

"Are you sure you want to go in?" he said.

"Absolutely," I said, looking up and down this animated cloak of vacuity.

"And are you sure that you're sure?" he said.

At this point, I was becoming somewhat irritated with this inane confirmation quiz.

"Dammit! I mean to say that, with your permission, I want to go in and have a look," I said.

"Well, okay then," said BT.

BT instructed me to stand about an arm's length from the wall, and then stare into it. The wall had little glints of luminous mineral flakes within it. As I stared into it, the glints within began moving, forming lines of waves, undulating in formations reminiscent of waves in a river with winds and cross currents. The waves were forming complex patterns that traveled from left to right, yet intermingling with other waves simultaneously moving from right to left. This was an intrinsically ambiguous motion. Its direction depended on how one looked at it.

BT said, "If you still want in, then concentrate on the left-to-right waves. And if at any time you want out, then concentrate on the right-to-left waves."

Concentrating on the left-to-right waves, I sustained this attention for a minute or so. Nothing was happening. I turned about to ask BT if I were doing it wrong, but this question soon became moot.

Turning around, I expected to see BT to my right and the other two on my left, and the truck between them. This is how they were, but this was not now the case. Instead, BT appeared to my left and the other two on my right. Straight ahead was a spacious auditorium with a high ceiling, maybe fifty feet up and made of monolithic granite. In front of me stood two rows of shadow beings, each row consisting of about two dozen members.

Their attire was not like the oversized robes of the others, but formed a more articulated fit, more like a jumpsuit than a curtain. They were all lined up, motionless, like soldiers standing at attention.

Overlooking this surface was a mezzanine enclosed in plates of glass. Behind it stood a multitude of "spectator" shadow beings. On the ground floor where I was standing, several corridors led away from the main auditorium, each one having a large square entrance, each one leading away in its own direction, each one fading away into its own mysterious darkness.

I awoke to find myself staggering and struggling to stand up on an undulating floor. I kept falling over. It was as nauseating as a daredevil carnival ride. The "floor" was moving like the sea, yet it was solid. With some practice, I acquired my sea-legs. The project of learning how to stand up in this crazy room had temporarily distracted my attention from a far more serious hazard.

Incredibly, it was raining jagged shards of glass. If I weren't already dead, I would have surely died then, torn to shreds by the downpour of brittle daggers. But I was undamaged. I held out my hand to catch a fragment. It sliced right through my hand without resistance, blood, or injury. This was baffling.

As I obtained some steadiness, I had more opportunity to look around. Across the room was a bench of solid granite. It was not undulating like the main floor, rather it had its own independent floor. Behind this stood a shadow-being wearing an oversized robe like Bent Triangle. He reflected no light at all, yet he radiated a demeanor that identified himself as a unique character. I got the feeling he had been waiting for me. He stood adjacent to a screen of about four feet by four feet.

"Four Squares," he said, introducing himself.

He was "pointing" to an object on the screen: I thought he was asking me if I could recognize the image. The chart was a black field with white dots. It looked like a night sky. The chart kept changing, about every two seconds displaying a new scene.

FS kept pointing and asking, "This one? This one? This one?. . ."

The chart was changing uncomfortably fast; his insistence was irritating. The attention demanded by the chart was competing with the attention needed just to stand up while simultaneously trying to deal with the shower of glass fragments. I didn't even know whether it was really a star chart at all. It was incredible that any being in the universe could be so casually attending a chart, yet so oblivious to the obvious hazards presented by the chaos of their immediate environment. It was confounding. But then a scene flashed by that seemed familiar.

"That one," I said.

It superficially looked like the constellation Hercules when viewed westward from a low latitude. I could even see the great Hercules globular cluster, M13. It was hard to understand FS. He didn't have the communication skill of BT, but he seemed to be saying that all the scenes were of the same object but viewed from different perspectives. He pointed to a particular "star." If my amateur astronomy knowledge was correct, and if this were actually a star chart, then the subject star of his reference would have been "Pi Hercules", or something nearby. I could not grasp what he was trying to tell me about it, only that this object was important. Why? To whom? In what sense? I couldn't understand.

I awoke standing in a granite corridor. It was about ten feet high and eight feet wide; its length was beyond estimate. All the corners were square. I looked around for the "crazy room," but it was completely gone. I couldn't see any rooms. Then BT showed up and signaled me to accompany him.

"Musician is amazed. He wants to visit you but is afraid," BT said with hushed discretion."Don't make any scary moves, this is his first encounter with an alien, and we don't want to damage his confidence."

On reaching Musician's station, his psychic field radiated absolute terror yet intense curiosity and interest in alien music. I wondered if he could sense how amazed I was.

After a pause of confusion, he handed me his native instrument in a reaching motion that maximized the distance between us. Very, very slowly, I reached out to take the recorder. It was very light. I think it was made of plastic. I stood there making no further moves. Musician was the only one of the crew that I'd observed that wore an overt space-suit. It was a bulky white outfit with a silvery dome on top. Maybe he felt more secure in its protection.

For a while, we just stood there in silence. Then, after a deliberate hesitation, he began to carefully communicate.

"We too have your kind of wind instrument," he said. "But in ours, the alto and tenor are united, separated by a 'wave trap.' The alto fingering is the same as yours. The tenor fingering is exactly opposite yours. And the trap knows whether you mean to play alto or tenor."

He then asked me to play chromatic scales without skipping a beat, starting with the tenor, then continuing up through the alto, and then back down the scale to tenor.

"That's a total of four octaves and eleven stops," I thought. "This could be a challenge."

The opposite fingering routine halfway through required a conscientious concentration. It took a little practice. Gradually, I could kind of do it, but four octaves of the chromatic scale with trick fingering was laborious. I played the scales a few times the best I could. I was thankful for his patience.

Amazingly, the note intervals seemed familiar. I had often speculated about the universality of scales. I played the scales again and again, but I was getting tired of the endeavor. So, just for relief, I played "Wild Wood Flower" by J.P. Webster, an easy folk melody I knew well; it was the first piece I ever learned in the slammer.

Musician seemed bewildered but less scared. I returned his instrument. I hoped I'd made a good impression. My mind was too suppressed to think clearly enough to ask him to play his melody. Although, later on, I heard what I thought may have been indigenous "singing."

Someone was calling me. I turned away from Musician and began walking the corridor, trying to trace the source of the signal. As I walked along, the corridor became increasingly narrow, and the walls began to fade away until they were nothing. It was as if I were walking along a narrow isthmus suspended in space. This is when two shadow-beings approached me from beyond the isthmus. They had the bearing of big city surgeons on a Saturday night.

"We'll be taking your materiality now," the one said in a very matter-of-fact voice.

"What?" I said."This is preposterous!"

What came to mind was a box of ashes.

"Oh, no, you don't!" I said.

I decided to punch this guy as hard as I could and make a run for it. But my body became paralyzed. My body was seized. My limbs tied down, spread-eagle, onto a large ring, as if I were a hide to be dried and cured. Then an electric jolt changed everything. NZZZSST!

Then I was then standing on the upper balcony of an anatomical theater, looking down at myself stretched out across the ring. I was the only spectator amongst the concentric rings of granite seats. I wondered if this was to be the end of me. God only knew what they planned to do next. I couldn't watch. I just ran away down the adjacent corridor. I noted how running was so easy with my newfound mass-less structure. This all the more confirmed the atrocity that had just taken place.

Slowing down, the shame of running away became unbearable. If I were to be true to myself, I needed to stop and conjure up the courage to go back and somehow recapture my materiality. I turned about, but the way back had vanished. It was just an empty corridor. I turned and continued walking along in the original direction. As I walked along this long gray corridor of granite, I became increasingly determined to find myself.

I was alone in a very long, quiet corridor inside a solid granite monolith. Its corners were all square, and its height and width looked to be about twelve feet both ways. Its distal ends extended indefinitely into a remote darkness. Yet, wherever I walked, a diffuse illumination followed. It was a long and lonely walk, nothing but granite and solitude. I thought it might never end.

But then I noticed curious niches randomly stationed along the walls. At first, they were small, at a few cubic inches each. But as I continued along, the niches became increasingly larger. Eventually, niches appeared that were large enough to be spacious parlors of thousands of cubic feet. The floors of these niches were sometimes even with the corridor floor, but some were displaced up or down by varying distances. Sometimes inches, sometime feet. I couldn't imagine why any architect would build such a nonsensical edifice. Then, one of these niches called to me.

I entered the calling niche. It was a small dark room illuminated mainly by the green glow of an upright instrument. The instrument was about three feet tall and four feet wide; it was mounted on a dark granite bench. Luminous vertical strings spanned its height. It looked to me like a glowing zither. Just then, Bent Triangle appeared.

"Indeed, this is a zither. It has fifty-four strings, and each string is a different element," he said.

"That doesn't make any sense," I said. "Why would the strings all be different elements?"

BT said, "The important thing for you to remember is that it has fifty-four strings. Play it."

With skeptical reserve, I looked over the instrument. The strings looked all the same to me even if they were all different, all fifty-four of them. I touched one, and it emitted sound. Soon I discovered they played by touch, not by pluck. Trying different strings, I could find no order in its tuning. The notes were randomly arranged. Trying to play this thing generated a cacophony of dissonant sound, hard on the ears of any species. After considerable experimentation, I found three strings that played together as a harmonious chord.

"This chord. It's the best I can do given my expertise," I said.

I awoke walking along the corridor. A niche with an especially wide entrance caught my attention. I stopped and observed an odd assemblage. There were rows and rows of shadow-beings, each standing before a shadow lectern, each one busily concentrating on their respective lecterns. It reminded me of a huge office room, except all the workers were standing instead of seated. One caught my attention.

She was especially strange, though I cannot remember why. I must have been staring too intensely. She did not speak, but rather radiated an irritated disapproval. The surface of her robe began to glow with a white grid on its surface. She looked like a paper-mache figure made of negative graph paper. I didn't mean to bother them, whatever they were doing, so I backed away. As I did so, the graph paper image faded away and the hue of her robe returned to its normal shadowiness.

Seeking my materiality, I had no idea how to recognize it, or how to put it back on even if I found it. But it was mine; they'd had no right to seize it. If I was still alive, I had to find it and take it back. Continuing along the corridor, the search brought me to another niche. It was just wide enough to be an entrance.

"Maybe it's in there," I thought.

⇥ ⇤

I walked into a large and deserted conference room. On either side of the main aisle were several rows of granite seats. The front of this room was empty, as if it were a space reserved for a speaker or some kind of display. I walked toward the front of this room, all the while scanning for myself, not knowing what to expect. Then a shadow man just appeared. He was carrying a small artifact that he handed to me. It was a silver cube about an inch on each side.

"In this world there is a puzzle," he said."You can have the prize inside if you can open it."

I looked at this cube very carefully. I wondered how this thing could be opened, as it had no seams or indents or buttons; it was solid silver. I looked closely. While studying the artifact, my peripheral vision alerted me to a deformation in the wall ahead. I looked up to see that a small cubic depression had appeared in the wall. It began to grow. It grew and grew until it formed a large cubical niche of about eight feet in all dimensions, its floor about three feet above the main floor.

"What a bizarre development," I thought.

As I looked into this niche, there suddenly appeared two figures standing on its surface, one slightly taller than the other. Unlike the ultra-blackness of the other shadow-beings, these two wore silky robes of vivid colors. Broad bands of blue, black, gold, red, and white clung to their feminine shape. Each stripe was about four inches wide and formed opposing diagonals meeting along a vertical center line at right angles, thus forming a large chevron or herringbone pattern of colors. Oversize sleeves hung over their wrists hiding what would be their hands.

The length of this robe extended from neck to floor. Their heads were enclosed in cubes decorated with broad colorful stripes. Instead of a chevron, these stripes formed an "asterisk" that covered the entire cube.

The posture of these two figures formed a partial crouched position, their knees and elbows partially bent. Their movements were a synchronous swaying, twisting action. It was if they were dancing the "twist," but in slow motion. As they twisted, they emitted slow harmonious tones synchronous with their motion. As their bodies slowly twisted in this crouched position, the silky robes revealed the impressions of knee caps gliding along underneath. It was becoming increasingly difficult to concentrate on the puzzle cube.

I became conscious. I found myself seated on a granite bench in a granite room, illuminated by that same diffuse lighting that characterized so much of this castle. One shadow man was seated to my left, another to my right. Before us was a granite table. On the opposite end of the table, Bent Triangle was seated on his own bench. It was a small room of about eight feet wide and eight feet deep. Its granite walls extended upward about twenty feet to the ceiling. The room had two entrances that opened up to perpendicular directions; that is, the room stood at the corner of intersecting corridors. From my perspective, looking toward the open entrances, I could see that the walls were quite thick at about four feet. For several minutes, we all just sat there in stillness and silence.

Then, Bent Triangle handed me a cylinder. I handled it carefully, not knowing what it was. I turned it and inspected it from different sides. It was about the size of a kaleidoscope. But like the shadow-beings themselves, it reflected no light. It was a shadow-cylinder, except for one square patch of blue.

"What is this object?" BT asked.

Slowly, I turned it over again. The blue patch looked like a large postage stamp. Looking close, I could see the details of an image. In the center of the blue patch, black lines depicted a rectangular shape with a curved top. It looked like an archway. Under the arching top was another arching line, but with horizontal segments on each end. The space within the archway was otherwise empty.

On the lower left and right edges of this rectangle were short diagonal lines. They reached up from the corners, almost touching the central archway. Midway along each line were two lobes extending outward from the central line. They looked like butterfly wings, or maybe radiation patterns of a dipole antenna. Little triangles were drawn at each outer corner of the patch. In their multitude, they overlapped each other and sometimes merged with small elongated rectangles drawn along the edge of each of the four sides of the patch. I pressed the patch as if were a button, but nothing happened. I could not guess its function, if any.

As I inspected the rest of the cylinder, I noticed that the vista from immediately over its top seemed to distort the background scene. It was as if a non-reflecting lens were attached to the end of the cylinder. This was curious. I pitched the cylinder over in order to look directly into the top. Inside was the appearance of a darkness blacker than black. This was more than a shadow-object. It was "actively" black. The sight of it was pulling my eyes out. It inflicted the kind of pain one feels when looking into too bright a light; it was the pain of intense light but without the light.

Immediately, I looked away and aimed the cylinder at the ceiling. Just to be sure, I took another quick look into the aperture. I experienced a pain like looking into the sun, but this was an absolute darkness, or perhaps a negative light. I blinked, then I carefully handed the cylinder back to BT, being careful not to aim it at him.

"I have no idea what this is, but I think it might be dangerous," I said.

⊯ ⊱

I found myself walking along a wide corridor, trying to think of a strategy that would evade the hospitality of my captors and enable me to locate and steal back my own materiality. Walking along this granite hallway, I came upon a little shadow being. I thought it might be a child. He was sitting on the floor, playing with tiles and blocks. I said nothing, but walked well around thinking it best to keep a safe distance between us. His mama, wherever she was, could become aggressive if I intruded too close to Junior's space. I was startled when he began communicating with perfect clarity.

"Stop worrying about your materiality," he said."They only borrowed it. They took it to the 'ice place' and soon enough, they'll bring it back and re-install it. So stop worrying about it."

Then he requested I keep his communication secret. He was not supposed to talk to me at all. His message was appallingly strange. I couldn't say anything. I didn't mean to be rude; I should have thanked him, but the bizarreness of the encounter left me speechless. I backed away and continued the quest.

⇥⊹⊹⇤

The corridor became increasingly wide. Eventually it led to an open lobby with several connected rooms, each with large square accesses separated by low partitions, each one facing a common desk. It reminded me of a bank lobby, but in monolithic granite.

Someone called me. The voice seemed to come from a room within the lobby, but when I entered, the room turned out to be an open arena. When the voice called again, I realized it emitted from a large cube nested inside the arena. It looked about thirty feet in each dimension. It had a single square entrance just wide enough for me. Looking in, I noticed the walls were as thick as the entrance itself. Subdued lighting shown throughout. I stepped in, but then I had to abruptly stop.

There, in the corner of the room, stood a profoundly curvaceous Shadow Woman. She had the figure of a prehistoric Venus one might see in a fine arts museum, only in ultra-black and very alive. I thought it best to suppress the growing urges of primitive attraction. I didn't understand what these beings were, or what their mores, or customs, or etiquette might be.

"Be seated," she said.

Two cubical benches were positioned at either end of a long central bench. These benches seemed to be made of slate rather than granite. The lower central bench reminded me of a coffee table. At each end, a shiny glass square nested in its own station like a window on a doily. One white, the other black. They were about one foot squared.

As I sat down, Shadow Woman walked over toward me. Her gait flowed like the shadow of an afternoon cloud drifting along a summertime meadow. She stopped next to the opposing bench.

"Let's play a game," she said in a calm and relaxed voice.

"Hmmm ... " I thought.

She alluded to the squares and said, "Each chamber contains a psychic essence, one white, the other black. There's a hidden connection between them. The squares will connect us. . ."

"Connect us?" I asked, looking up.

She said, "The object of the game is to collect the most of the sum. And the only rule is that the rate of flow must be inversely proportional to what is left."

I wanted to cooperate, but I really didn't understand the concept of this game. I was about to ask for clarification. But the atmosphere had changed.

A feeling of suspense came over me. The air became charged with intense expectation. It felt like the moment just before a symphonic performance. Then she moved!

Enchanted, I watched as this ample body of rippling topography straddled the opposing bench. She had the bearing of a pagan temple and the mood of a rising tide. Waves of wildness swept through my nerves. Winds of boldness whistled through my ears. And a mysterious illumination surprised my eyes as the glowing hue of kneecaps materialized through her shadowy motif.

"What is this?" I said.

The glowing hue began to grow and spread further and further. Like dawn's earliest hints, the nascent rays of a heavenly aura slowly revealed a novel frontier. Rolling hills and delicate valleys began to appear. Flashes of distant sparkles slithered in synchronous rhythms. Trembling currents of an adventurous sea reached out to the shores of a wandering consciousness, only to retreat in a dangerous undertow pulling its way back to an inner realm of shadowy mystery. And then...

OH! GOD! Suddenly a bedazzling vista of ethereal paradise flashed through my senses. Stunned by the beam of ultimate destiny, its radiance flushed my head and astounded the core of my being. I was nearly breathless.

Then her presence became intense. Apprehension loomed in my head as she spoke with words incomprehensible. Her complexion became a haze of gray, marbled with gold and purple strata. Her whole body began floating and undulating. Then she was hovering above like a cloud in a gathering storm. Restless winds began to rotate. My hair stood on end as if she were electrified and poised to pounce in a thunderous discharge. Her body heat was all over me. Then I felt her breath on my face!

Suddenly, a tornadic pull grabbed my head. I tried to pull back, but her coiling grip just squeezed tighter. I could feel her heart beating, its temperature rising with each beat. Writhing contortions surged through her body. Moaning tectonics reverberated through her quivering voice. Then her heart began pounding like a racing locomotive coming right towards me. Faster and faster, its power shook the ground with ever more ferocity. Electrified panic curled my toes.

"I can't take it anymore!" I screamed in desperation.

Crash! A bolt of lightning exploded my balance. It was like slipping up on ice, but protracted as if it would never end. I could feel the essence flowing between the chambers. Faster and faster, the flow kept accelerating. I tried to resist, but her suction was too powerful.

Then her churning convulsions became violent. I was thrown about like a kayak in the rapids. Storms of foam blustered in all directions. My ears began ringing with a squealing cry. She kept screaming as the roaring vortex consumed my head and collapsed my skull. My whole body was being devoured and turned inside out.

Then quiet. In a slow-motion stupor, I found myself hopelessly lost in the swirling depths of a cosmic maelstrom. I thought I was dead.

I awoke and sat up and found myself on the coffee table. As my blurred vision came into focus, I struggled to recall the purpose of the game.

"The sum . . . to collect . . . the squares. . ." I thought. "Yes, the squares . . . I should assess the status of the squares."

I looked about. But the squares . . . they had transformed into shiny cubes. And in their reflection . . . a shadowy likeness of an alien smile appeared before slowly fading away. My heart skipped a beat.

I took a minute to catch my breath. I looked again. I could see that the white and black cubes had completely interchanged. All that had been white was now black. All that had been black was now white. I guessed she won.

Not wanting to be a sore loser, I said, "Good game," as if I had understood any of this.

In a long pause of bewilderment, Shadow Woman stared at me from the opposing bench, her ultra black figure still as a statue.

Finally she said, "The purpose of the game is to collect the most of the sum, but the sum is always constant. So there cannot be any winners, nor any losers."

"What a peculiar game," I thought."I should have asked her name."

I awoke to find myself walking the corridor, searching for my materiality. A placard on the wall caught my attention. It was a white field with black dots. The dots formed an elongated "S." A chart like this usually depicted main sequence stars, but this one had a secondary elongated "S," only shorter and within the zone of white dwarf stars. I didn't think any such relationship existed. Perhaps this glyph didn't even represent stars. Maybe I was looking at it wrongly. I tried looking at different angles when I began to feel that uneasy staring sensation. I turned about face. Bent Triangle was standing there. His psychic radiance signaled disapproval. I was not supposed to be in this area. Thus far, my host's containment of what to them was an alien specimen had been incredibility permissive, but it seemed there were limits to my expeditions.

"If you were in my shoes, unwillingly exported to an utterly strange environment, wouldn't you too explore as much as you could?" I asked defensively.

Error. There occurred an error in communication. For a moment, BT seemed puzzled. Then his attitude changed from disapproval to one of humor. I could hear his thoughts.

He thought I was asking him, "How would you compare yourself to me?"

He laughed and said, "About nine hundred thousand years beyond Sun Tzu."

Then he "pointed" to one of his associates . He was hunched over a bench in what seemed to be a small shop in a niche about ten feet above the main floor.

BT laughed and said, "Except for him, HSSS. He thinks that he is a million years beyond Sun Tzu."

"How does BT know about Sun Tzu?" I wondered.

BT signaled for me to follow him. We walked a long way, finally arriving at the farthest station. This room had several aisles separated by long granite benches. The room formed a "T" shape with adjacent rooms attached to each end of the "T," their interiors mostly obfuscated by a maze of intervening walls. It had the ambiance of a machine shop.

Seated on the long bench next to the entrance was a middle-aged human of Latino ethnicity. I was surprised. Until now, I had not seen any other of my own species. I wondered who he was and why he was here. He seemed to be semiconscious, just sitting there, breathing but inanimate.

BT gestured to this being and asked me the following: "Is this you, or are you related to him, or do you know him?"

I looked at the guy again. I had no idea who he was.

I said, "No, none of those."

BT then led me farther along the aisle beside the long, granite bench. BT slowed and stopped. I trailed along ever more slowly. I could see it was another human, and it was beginning to look familiar. I wasn't sure if I wanted to see this.

"Oh, God no, I think this is going to be me," I said with irrational dread.

With an authoritative voice, BT asked me the same question: "Is this you, or are you related to him, or do you know him?"

I looked, I looked away, I looked again. I was shocked.

Seated there before me was my own body. I was overwhelmed. I had been searching for my materiality all day, and now it was right there. But the exotic dissonance of being the observer and the observed at the same time was quite unnerving. My body sat in a slouched posture, eyes half closed, mouth half open. It looked like a retard on Thorazine. I stooped down to look more critically at this corporeal entity, its features all too familiar.

"That's me," I thought.

I stooped farther to look directly into the eyes. They were much lighter than normal. The iris consisted of black spokes on a background of light gray, the pupils severely constricted. I began to wonder what kind of thing I could be that observed itself as a detached entity.

"Is this you, or are you related to him, or do you know him?" BT asked again.

"Is this me. . . ?" I thought. "What a stupid question."

I was about to say, "Yes, that's obviously me."

"But maybe not . . . think about this," I said to myself. "BT must already know that this is my body, my constellation of traits, my DNA, my papers. After all, it's his crew that had stolen it. This is ridiculous. So why is he asking? What's this about anyway?"

Either natural or artificial, my claims to having an identity had all been based on a bundle of traits, or tags, or possessions attached. All artifacts that alluded to something that was never named.

"None of these are literally the 'self' itself," I said to myself. "So what is?"

"If I were to attempt to cite an 'essential self' apart from this constellation of traits and tags that normally passes as 'self,' then I would first have to subtract all these traits and tags," I thought to myself. "But what would be left? Nothing?"

I had spent all day searching for my "material existence." Now I was searching for my "self-essence."

"Maybe my 'self' is a metaphor and nothing more. A myth conjured up by a bucket of wet clay," I said to myself.

The thought of my non-reality began to secrete a veil of dark depression.

In a liminal state of surreal bafflement, I had to wonder, "What am I really about, if anything?"

Then... I remembered something Ivan had said long ago: ". . .About! It isn't here...it's always going to be, maybe..."

A vision appeared before me: It was Dozer. He was carrying a chewed-up veil as he jumped right through an attic door from the inside out. A sudden awareness of being flooded over me.

"I am . . . 'always going to be, maybe,'" I said to myself.

I stood there for some time trying to sort out some kind of framework that could possibly express an answer to BT's question.

I realized then there couldn't be an objective answer. The "self" seeking the "self" is a thing intrinsically indeterminate. An unknowable thing about to be. I stood at attention and attempted to answer, the best I could, whether or not this corporal was myself. I answered with all my sincerity.

"Who knows who we really are?" I said.

BT staggered backwards and radiated a blast of incoherent laughter. He seemed to think that was really, really funny. I didn't think this was so funny. This was a serious issue, a novel inquiry. I had given it my most careful consideration. BT calmed down and regained his composure. Then he gestured to the Latino guy.

"You really are related to him," he said.

Then the lights went out.

My ears were popping as I became aware that I was standing in a small, stuffy room with a large window and a low ceiling. The lights were dim, as if I were in a closet illuminated only by flashlight. I steadied myself against the wall, as I was somewhat dizzy. I discovered I had my materiality back. I wondered where I might be. I looked at the walls. They were not the granite that characterized the castle.

"Must be outside," I thought.

The window was rectangular, about two feet high and four feet wide with rounded corners. I leaned in close.

Outside, as far as I could see left and right, there hung a stack of rainbows against an otherwise black environment. I moved from side to side to get a sense of range, but they were too far away to perceive any parallax or to get any idea of their distance. There were six or seven of these rainbows, horizontally oriented and all slightly bowed downward, pointing to a common center. For a short time, I stood in amazement looking at the rainbows. But I really wanted to know where I was. I stood on my toes with my head against the window looking down, searching for a landmark, a beacon, or any clue as to my present position. Then my sight, my attention, and my consciousness all faded away.

I awoke to find myself in the truck. I had no idea where I was, or how I got there, or what had been happening the previous day. I looked out the windshield, then scanned the instruments. I was on an interstate road in a clear, moonless night, traveling at highway speed, cruise control on, headlights on, oil pressure, temperature, and voltage all nominal. Fuel on full. It was twelve o'clock midnight.

I became aware that I was speaking out loud.

"I'm the only one on this road, and it's been that way all along. I'm the only one on this road, and it's been that way all along."

I kept reiterating this mantra until I began to wonder why. But the inquiry vanquished this automatic speech.

Then the pungent smell of gasoline filled the cab. That I could detect the smell of gasoline at highway speed meant there must have been a major fuel leak under the hood.

"This is dangerous. I should pull off the road immediately and be ready to run away in case of explosive fire," I thought.

I had stowed a fire extinguisher and a hose repair kit behind the seat.

"If I can fetch the extinguisher in time, maybe I can save the truck and fix the leak," I said to myself.

But being stopped on an interstate road at night carries its own risk. Just then, I saw the "Rest Stop 1 Mile" sign.

"Maybe traveling the extra mile to pull into the safety of the rest stop, away from the interstate at night, would outweigh the risk of fire in the extra minute of travel. But maybe not," I thought.

Before I could decide the best move, something ahead demanded my attention. About a mile ahead and somewhat to the left of the road, I witnessed the ascent of a small, pastel, off-white orb. It was about the size of a pea viewed at arm's length. It gently traveled upward, then leveled out at about five hundred feet above ground. Then it came toward me. I rolled down the window. It reminded me of something I had seen at the mom-and-pop airport where I worked. Sometimes at night, I would sit on the picnic table watching students doing "touch and go practice" at night. I had seen this picture before.

"Must be an airport over there somewhere. Someone's taking off toward me along a runway parallel to the road. Wonder where he's going?" I thought.

Looking down a runway, landing lights would seem to ascend, then level off until they reached climb speed. But as this orb drew closer, its diameter became larger but not brighter. The light was too smooth, too round, too mellow. It didn't have the glare or vibration one would expect from aircraft landing lights. And it wasn't climbing. This wasn't looking right.

The orb continued parallel to the road coming closer, getting larger. As it became close, I could see it from an angle instead of head-on. It was somewhat elliptical rather than round as I'd first thought. Then I noticed that it was dropping off smaller orbs as it went, one about every three seconds. The little orbs would travel down to about halfway to the ground, then vanish. Then another, the same way.

The main orb was drawing close. It now had the angular size of an egg viewed at arm's length, while the little orbs appeared the size and color of pearls. It made no sound. This was not an airplane, nor a helicopter, nor a hot-air balloon, nor an advertisement dirigible.

"So . . . what is that?" I said to myself.

The orb was just about to pass me as we traveled in opposite directions, and then it was directly to my left, abeam of the truck. That was when it spoke.

It said quite clearly, "Never forget the delusion of UFO, we'll be right back."

"This doesn't make any sense at all," I thought.

I watched it over my left shoulder as it traveled away along the road. I was at highway speed and could only afford a few seconds of backward watching. I turned to look straight ahead.

"Rest Area Next Stop," read the sign.

The rest stop had no buildings, no facilities, no lighting. Everything was dark, only starlight. It was just a utility pavement off the main road. I pulled in and stopped. Looking behind me, I could still see the main orb traveling away and the little orbs dropping down.

"This is certainly a curious sight," I thought to myself. "Indeed. As a matter of fact, this is an unbelievable sight. Wait a second! This is an astonishing sight! Could this possibly be? Dare I even suspect against all conceivable odds?"

The possibility of alien contact would be beyond fantastic. This was a once in a lifetime opportunity. I couldn't miss this. I grabbed a flashlight and a monocular. I was going to blink "Hello" and then "SH5" in Morse code and see if they would reply. The excitement was nearly unbearable.

("SH5" in Morse code, 3-4-5, is astronomer J. Allan Hynek's concept of an interstellar communication flag. It alludes to integral values of a right triangle geometry knowable to intelligent species.)

I exited the truck with the flashlight in one hand and the monocular in the other. I was about to signal the white orb, but as I got out of the truck, I was surprised to see a red orb sitting on the ground just across road, opposite from the rest stop. I couldn't understand how I could have possibly missed it as I'd pulled into the utility road.

"It must have just now appeared," I said in amazement.

This red orb had an angular size of a baseball viewed at arm's length, and its red color came in two shades. It was really two concentric spheres. The inner sphere was a light, bright red with a sharply sketched perimeter. The outer sphere was a dark, deep red with a fuzzy outline.

"What can this possibly be?" I thought. "I'll have to investigate this."

I was afraid, but I wanted to know more. This was a phenomenon too extraordinary to neglect.

"This is worth the risk, whatever it is," I said to myself. I started towards it.

I became frozen. I could not move anything. Then I perceived a presence next to me in the darkness. I could not see it; rather, it was a radiance felt.

Then a strange voice spoke: "Don't look at the red one, it's too dangerous for you to see. But you can look at everything else."

Then I could move again. With mindless obedience, I turned away from the red orb and returned to the truck. The odor of gasoline was gone, but I could remember the urgency of the need to check out the fuel system. I looked under the hood at the fuel connections, then under the truck at the fuel filter and lines. Then I looked around the tank and the fill cap. Nothing.

While I had the lamp, I checked the oil, the belts, the tires, and everything else I could think of. I didn't find any obvious problems. I got back into the truck, and sat there for a while, just waiting. Just waiting. After all, they'd said they would be "right back."

I looked all around except toward the red one. The night was so dark. No city lights, no moon, no farm lights off in the distance. There was absolutely no traffic. Only vivid starlight on a severely clear sky over a flat, unobstructed land.

"This place is perfect for star-gazing," I thought.

I looked at the many stars and contemplated their stories, their joys, and their tragedies. I could see Leo and Arco and Virgo. The night was so clear that I could even see the "bee hive" cluster at the heart of Cancer with my naked eye.

"Let's see... From the position of these stars, I must be headed west," I thought. "And their declination would put me about forty-five degrees North latitude."

The February night was getting cold. And oddly, the alien presence became irrelevant. It was time to move on.

CHAPTER 6

THE ROAD THROUGH REPRESSION

I was driving west through the night on what seemed to be an interstate highway.

"Which one? Where? Why?" I thought.

There was absolutely no other traffic, no lights, no towns, no signs, and no clues. Just hours of driving. I had the uneasy feeling that I was the only person in this world.

"How do I survive a vacated world? What should I do next?" I wondered.

I drove on through the night for about three hours looking for any sign of civilization. Then a sign post: "Rapid City." Suddenly, there was heavy traffic. It looked like rush hour. Cars, pickup trucks, tractor-trailers, motorcycles all rushing by in the eastbound lane. Then the westbound lane suddenly became filled with its own rush hour traffic. I was certainly not alone. It was three o'clock in the morning. I pulled in to the next gas station for fuel. Checking the map, I located Rapid City and discovered which highway I had just been riding.

"Okay… I know where I am," I thought."Gillette would be just a little farther west."

On driving west beyond the big city at interstate speed, the traffic abated to less density. Relieved to discover civilization, I took a breath of relief. I was not alone. As this drive went on through the night, my mind began to wander.

"I just reviewed the plan for this trip while at Murdo, that little town two hundred miles behind me," I thought. "Left there mid-afternoon headed for Gillette. I'm almost there now. It's four o'clock in the morning. Makes perfect sense."

Pulling into Gillette, I checked in at the first motel at the edge of town. Waning moon's last sliver shone in through the stairwell window. It was strikingly clear against the dark sky of winter's morning. It was almost five o'clock.

Once in the room, I headed for the lavatory. I washed my hands and looked in the mirror. I was a bit of a mess. Tangled hair, wrinkled up shirt, and a discoloration in my face. It had a blue tint that reminded me of a chronic drunk I once knew. I could see the veins in my nose. But I had not been drinking at all. I washed my face. Blood in the sink. A slight nose bleed had infiltrated my mustache.

"Must be the dry air," I thought, "Hope I didn't offend the check-in clerk."

Wake up call rang in at 10 a.m. I had no recollection of the anomalous episode of the previous day and didn't care at all. I had left Murdo and now I was in Gillette; that was that.

I was at the sink shaving my chin as I had done every morning on the trip. This was a matter of routine and pride. But shaving this particular morning became more difficult than usual. It seemed my beard was two days old instead of one.

"Must have forgotten to shave yesterday," I said to myself.

After checking out of the motel, I rode down the street to a doughnut shop still serving breakfast. My head was in a fog. I sipped coffee. At the counter, I tried to read the headlines through the vending machine grill. The present edition was for tomorrow. It was dated for Monday but today was Sunday.

"I guess the paper boy's running a little ahead of time," I thought."No, that's not it. This is a leap year. February has an extra day, that's all."

Later that morning, I called Ivan letting him know I was just leaving Gillette. He reported the weather conditions in Oregon. Then he asked why I had not called the day before as I'd said I would.

"Well, Ivan is getting old, he probably gets confused," I thought.

I apologized. But none of this mattered. In fact, I shouldn't even think about it. I drove on through Wyoming, then Montana. I didn't think about anything. Miles passed. I stayed the night in a motel someplace. Maybe Idaho. Nothing mattered. But then, the next day I passed a road sign: "Oregon."

"Hey! Oregon! This is where I'm going," I said."Look at this beautiful country. Hey! I'm somebody. I'm here and now!"

After staying the night at Hotel Salem, I called Ivan for detailed directions. It was mid-morning by the time the dining hall waitress filled the thermos. Oil and tires and belts looked okay. Everything seemed normal. But as I set off, a strange feeling hovered over my head.

"Ivan knows something vital," it said.

CHAPTER 7
THE REUNION

Directions to Possum Trot seemed clear enough driving the state roads and county roads with conventional signs. But as I turned off the main road just past the post office, I began to wonder if I knew what I was doing.

I looked again at the directions scribbled on the back of my note pad: "Turn off to the dirt road just past the post office. Then turn left just past the Short Fuse Saloon. Then turn right on Seldom Seen Road. Then go to the end of the pasture with the broken fence. Turn right on the private road about a mile before you get to where the sawmill used to be. Don't worry about the 'private road' sign, as we have an easement, and then when you come to the fork just beyond the creek..." The rest was unreadable.

"Well, this is certainly comforting," I thought.

The map and the roads became increasingly divergent.

"Perhaps the surveyors had become lost," I thought."Glad I brought some survival gear."

I checked the directions again. I wished I'd been more specific. I drove slowly along a nameless lane, and then my eyes began following a nearby creek. A bridge appeared.

"There it is, the forked road just over the creek," I said."The ventilated sign post won't be much help though. With a little luck, maybe I'll make the correct turn."

It was about noon when I drove up to the end of the dirt road towards what I thought might be Ivan's place. A Deuce and a Half army truck with a chainsaw in the driver seat sat next to a BMW with a Packard hood ornament. Something told me I was on the right trail.

The ruts were getting too deep. I wished I had four-wheel drive. The remaining trek would have to be on foot. I slung my duffel bag over my shoulder and set off along the rough road. Deep in the woods of Oregon, squirrels and birds and unseen critters scampered along the moss coated limbs of native trees towering overhead. A chorus of natural voices relieved the soul of the tired banality of modern civilization.

I hoped I was moving in the right direction. The path seemed headed to the outer limits of the world. Ivan had warned me about the stealthy cougars that loved to eat humans. I checked my hunting knife, made sure it was handy. I trekked on through the forest.

I wanted this visit for its own sake, for old times. But at the same time, I wanted to discover the meaning of the true self.

"Who am I . . . really," I said to myself. "This has been the ultimate quest of my life. Ivan is a very spiritual artist and a free thinker. I need his insight. But he's also very sensitive. How can I ask?"

Tramping on through the woods, I began to wonder if I were lost. But then I heard the whining voices of machine tools at work. Then a staccato clatter of a bouncing bucket. It reminded me of the "tune up" period before a symphonic performance got underway.

Then silence. No machine sounds, no footsteps, not even the chirps of wildlife residence. I stopped at the edge of the tree-line to listen carefully.

Then I called out, "EYEEEVAN! Ivan! It's just me."

No answer. I could see his house, but it was as if no one was home. No movement, no lights, no sounds.

"That can't be, he must have just been here," I thought."Somewhere."

KA-POW!! A seismic polka jumped my feet. Clods of dirt flew in my face. Stunned at first, then I started to run away. But the howling laughter of a familiar voice signaled the aliveness of my favorite trickster. Ivan was here alright. I ducked behind a tree and looked around toward the forest. Like magic, the old geezer emerged out from a cloud of blue smoke.

"Hey, hey, hey, amigo!" he shouted, tramping along in big steps through brush and weeds and clinging burrs.

A deer hide jacket and possum skin cap revealed his pioneer persona for the day. The executive neck tie confirmed his contempt for the world of the conventional. His graying beard reminded me how easily time could drift away. I should have come years earlier.

"Just thought I'd check out my new rifle," he said catching his breath."Made it myself, even the powder. . . . Seems like it works. . . . I think. . . . Here, you try it."

I just looked at him with conflicted puzzlement. Dogs barked in the distance. Clouds of sulfur spiced the atmosphere.

"You crazy scallywag," I said.

As we walked along past the garden up to his house, I suddenly stopped. Somewhat startled I stared at the stone walls. In some way, they were reminiscent of something vaguely familiar.

"Isn't this the same design as your father's old place back in Ohio?" I said.

"Yeahaaa. . . .Had to do a little work on this one," Ivan said, looking over the stump of his missing finger.

Moss climbed the stone steps.

As I stepped inside, the aroma of burnt charcoal reminded me of Ivan's old stove in Ohio. I shouldn't have been surprised when I saw it there in the corner, its embers still warm from last night's fire.

Kitchen table creaked and thumped with the periodic thuds of a beer bottle roll. Sticky dough of tribal tortillas and stray puffs of emancipated flour squished out across the planks of the coarse grain table. A kerosene lamp supervised the show with the tottering steps of a drunken director. Woman had aged well in her natural beauty, proud in the authenticity of her independent spirit. Her homemade dress revealed a pantheist tone in her native skills.

The living room was an art gallery. A rough-cut cedar table held arrangements of arrow heads, pine cones, and figurines fashioned from parts of a dissected radio. A clay sculpture of a sitting dog secured the sketches of nomadic dragonflies.

Woman's musing gaze captured in oils hung above the living room mantel. All along the walls hung pastels and sketches. Salmons cruising a creek of delicate swirls and exotic flora. Zombie- people watching TV, but seen from a point of view inside the TV. Blank faces staring out over a metropolis of glowing tubes.

Squirrels out on a limb. Fir trees with pointy hats and green beards tending to herds of goats and human livestock. Ants looking up at overarching mushrooms. A crow standing on a fence post watching the sun set. An oil painting of a grizzly old pioneer reloading his flint lock hung next to the spring-wound Victrola.

Stepping in the den, a sketch caught my attention. Its subject barely discernible. A charcoal vignette without a frame hung by a thumbtack over the marble top table. Dark and ambiguous. Shadowy figures infiltrating along through a dark forest. "... Interesting..." I thought to myself.

Screen door slammed. Ivan walked in with a load of firewood.

"Knew you'd be back," he said scooting a bucket next to the stove.

A pastel of a big turtle on a river rock hung next to an antler rack of vintage rifles.

"Here's Uncle Curly," he said, pointing to a painting of a big Douglas fir tree.

Curly had a pointy hat made of tourist hide, and an over coat of branches barely concealing an armory of muskets. He was watching a fox by a stream as an old man fed the chickens. Another painting depicted homeless people in the street with wild flowers growing up through the fractured pavement and a girl with a strange smile standing next to a junk yard. Then a painting of wild turkeys surrounding a hobo camp littered with Wild Turkey Whiskey bottles. All original art, scattered along the walls amongst the spears and fetishes of lost Amazonian tribes.

"Here's my masterpiece," he said with the jocular voice of a pool hall shark.

A convertible of Carps with human faces driving out of the forest headed to an amusement park. The sign over the park said, "We sell happiness." Stands of Tree people looked on with befuddlement.

"What a strange contrast," I said.

Ivan studied his father's old pipe, rolling it over and over.

"You know... there's a rift in the species," he said, "There's not many..."

"Unfinished project," Ivan said taking a seat at the kitchen table between bags of flour and a hand-crank coffee grinder.

A shirt button, a beer bottle cap, a thimble, a marble, and a machine nut, all laid out along a canvas as if pieces of an obscure puzzle.

"Crows leave it in the bird bath," he said, rolling over a small piece of stained glass. "They say they find these things all over the world. Haven't figured out how it goes together. Maybe I'll see it a dream. But the frame . . . now there's a one of a kind. Carved from absolutely positively genuine guaranteed stolen fence post with its very own certified bullet hole."

"You knew I'd be back?" I said.

Ivan got up with a surge of pride.

"Come on out back. Show you my workshop. Built it myself few years back," he said.

Walking out the back door, I thought something looked familiar.

"Ivan, that siding. . ." I said, looking up and down the gray timbers of the board and batten shed.

"Yeahaaa…. It's what was left after the storm back east. Still have Dozer's collar," he said with a stoic sadness."Built a special frame, hung it in the den next to the Banjo wall clock."

"This old car. Isn't that the same '39 Plymouth you had in Ohio?" I said.

"Salvage yards, flea markets, machine shops. Replaced about every part. The same? What a coup," he said sarcastically.

Stepping inside, I was greeted by a piece of sheet metal hanging by a rope. The painting twirled as I walked by. One side held the front of a terrible beast. The other side showed the disgusting back end.

"Beazles," Ivan said. "Cross between a bear and a weasel. Town's full of 'em."

Walking on past the work benches for jewelry and sculpting and machining, I ducked a light bulb hanging by its wires.

"Now here's a real Plymouth," he said, pointing to a large painting across the shop.

I was amazed by the extreme detail. Armed sailing ships from across the sea were headed for land. In the foreground, fir trees with pointy hats and long beards stood at the ready with ornate muskets, decorated cannons, and a fancy catapult. Conflict was imminent. On the beach, a peculiar rock seemed to stand out. Stepping closer, the image became ambiguous. Then the rock became that old Plymouth.

"Hey, I thought it was a rock. Or is that the Plymouth?" I said turning about.

I felt a chill. Ivan was gone. In his place hung a painting of a closed attic door with a Necker cube engraved on the front.

"We all see our own rainbows. . ." said a gravelly voice emanating from the darkest corner of the shop.

Walking back to the house, I reached in my pocket and withdrew the silver crow pendent.

"Remember this one?" I said. "I still carry it for good luck."

"Hey, hey, hey, amigo. . . . Don't forget to recharge it once in a while," he said. "Just set it out under a full moon. I figured you was one."

"One?" I thought.

We tromped on past jagged piles of scrap iron and buckets of smooth river rocks. I stared at the ground as we walked back to the house. I had come to Ivan in search of insight.

"He's quite sensitive, and now I'm his guest. I don't want to press this issue too hard. But I want to know," I thought to myself.

As we sat down on the floor of the back room den, I tried to think of a good way to frame the question. Ivan reached for the mason jars and poured us some clear.

"You still play recorder?" he said as he picked up a guitar from the corner.

"Go ahead man, I'll just sip and listen," I said.

Ivan tugged his beard then tinkered with a few impromptu chords. He kept looking at me with that midway pitchman look. I knew he wanted me to play along.

"Ivan, I like to hear you play but really, it's not any genera I know," I said.

He kept looking with that furtive grin.

"Oh well. Okay then... somehow," I said, reaching into my duffle bag for the pear-wood recorder.

As I started to assemble the instrument, I felt a vague fear and confusion. It was like I wasn't really present.

"I'm not supposed to think about this," I thought.

Just picking up the recorder seemed a momentous feat. I held the instrument to preheat the wood. For a moment, I felt as if I were moving in slow motion. I held tightly the tenor recorder.

"Must be feeling the fatigue of a long trip," I thought. " But my mission; I must try."

"Ivan, remember years ago, back in Ohio, when we used to talk about the meaning of 'self-essence'?" I said.

Ivan strummed a weird chord, seemed to be major and minor at the same time.

"Boy. . . .There's a new one on me," he said.

"What do you call that?" I asked.

He strummed another chord. This one sounded somewhat Latin yet aboriginal, congenial, but with a rouge dissonance just below the surface. Sub-audible beat notes rolled around the resonator like waves in an alien fjord.

"Beats me. Here, just play along... it doesn't matter," he said.

I knew I couldn't.

"Just play what you don't know. That's how Miles does it," he said.

I listened for a while. I tried to play what I thought was the prominent key. Then I tried to imitate the melody line, but it kept changing unexpectedly. I couldn't really follow what he was doing. Yet, whatever I did play, his voice answered mine in just the right way. Then my voice inspired a novel reply. An autonomous improvisation just grew up out of nowhere.

"Hey!" I said."It played itself!"

Ivan turned and looked far, far away out the open door through the mossy limbs of what was left of Earth's forests.

Then a somber voice said: "... Play it again..."

I blew the water out the recorder.

"Ivan, I really have no idea how it went," I said.

"So, so, so amigo. . . . Maybe it's beyond your idea," he said, reaching up the wall for another instrument.

"Lightning struck birch wood. Saw it when it hit. Nearly blinded me. Neighbor man traded me goat skin for a scrimshaw of his Harley Davidson. Hard part is getting it stitched and tuned. It's sensitive to everything. Shaman's drum will connect you," he said looking over the instrument.

". . .Connect me?" I whispered to myself.

For some reason, I felt an uneasy dread. Ivan looked up and stared out at a blank canvas. Its pine frame hanging unobtrusively over the cathedral radio.

"Everything's connected," he said.

For a while I just stared at the blank canvas.

After a long pause I said, ". . .Ivan, about the 'self'. . ."

"Here, check out my mbira," he said.

He began playing the little organ with his thumbs. Its simple rhythm bounced like rain drops falling in the forest. Its libertine melody flew like butterflies dancing in summertime dreams."Plywood leftovers from the roof," he said, as sensitive hands glided over its rough edges. I could see where he had engraved the soundboard.

"Wow, what a beautiful rose," I said."It's so delicate."

Ivan became serious and intent as he played the first phrase of "To a Wild Rose." By Edward MacDowell.

"What a talented guy," I thought.

Then he handed the instrument over to me.

"Anybody can play it," he said with a grin.

I looked at the crudely hammered out tongs, then my eyes drifted down to that beautiful engraving. Only now . . . I'm seeing it turned around . . .

"Oh, Ivan . . . that's obscene. . ." I said. "Wait, let me have another look."

"Haa . . . I know you can play that," he said. "Things aren't always what they seem."

Ivan got up and stretched out in an easy chair. I took the couch.

And then it was morning. The sun had traversed the sky without a night. Ivan wanted to show me something.

"Saw you there in a dream. . ." he said enigmatically. "It's a project I've been working on."

He put a polished brass around his neck and the drum under his arm. We set off into the woods. A cool brook of lively waters and ancestral rocks, Toli Creek flowed hidden under the shrouded canopy of willow trees. The aroma of Earth and Water filled the air. Little glints of sun rays peeked in through the branches.

"It doesn't have a beginning or an ending. It's the same creek, but it's never the same," he said, parting the branches of a fern.

We sat on the ground surrounded by moss. It was like a secret hideout. Ivan lit a joint. After a long pause, he said, "I know you've been seeking . . . you won't find it in Carp Man's world. It's in a different reality. Ever find your spirit guide?"

Ivan stationed the brass disk against a rock just under the surface.

"So, so, so, amigo. . . .What do you see?" he said.

Rippling waves of random currents and mutating patterns of refracted light distorted my image to the limits of recognition. It was if I were flowing somewhere.

"Is that me?" I said. "Ivan, I really can't tell what I'm looking at," I said.

Ivan cupped his hands over the mallet.

"It's not what you look at . . . it's what you see," he said sympathetically."If you're really seeking yourself, then you are seeking a self that seeks itself. It's your port to infinity, like this creek, like your dreams. Everything's connected. Just keep your question in mind."

Then the drumbeat started.

"Just tune it in," he said. "Tum Tum Tum Tum . . . ."

"Where is this going?" I wondered.

A regular beat. . . but then not quite so regular. . . then subtle variations began creeping in.

"Who am I? Who am I?. . ." I kept asking. "Tum Tum Tum Tum Tum Tum. . . ."

My head began ringing and resonating like the singing mantra of a waterfall. Then a rippling Mandala of flowing brass poured in through the in-finity of mirrors within mirrors. Roots and branches, birds and stars sailed by in rushing channels flow-ing up in a mist of stereo rainbows. Poly-rhythmic echoes flew on over the dreaming leaves and chaotic trails of a foreign jungle. Drum beats paced on like a prisoner on the run.

"Where am I going?" I wondered.

Crow landed on a Japanese maple just across the creek. Then Crow flew away. I tried to focus on the question.

"Ivan, I don't know how to do this," I said. "This is getting weird."

The drum slowed. Then only the subtle argot of a whispering creek could be heard.

". . . Comes with the wind, goes with the rain . . ." said a mindless voice gazing out through torrents of neutrinos raining in through the big window beyond the jungle.

A flash. Ivan's eyes lit up.

Then, in a voice of pristine innocence, he said, "Oh! ... I just saw it! Lucky you. It'll be in your dreams."

Returning to the cabin later that afternoon, I stood for several minutes studying a pastel of a zither. It was decorated with ornate spirals and exotic flowers.

"Where does Ivan get all these inspirations?" I wondered.

"Past lives," said Woman, walking by.

All the while in the back of my mind, I kept thinking about that weird safari earlier in the day. Ivan seemed so certain when he'd said, "It'll be in your dreams."

"What does that mean?" I wondered. "When would be the right time to ask?"

Ivan walked in from the backyard carrying buckets of water.

"I'll know it when it happens," he said.

As evening drifted toward night, we settled in on the hardwood floor of the back room den. I watched as Ivan began sorting through a basket of driftwood. Occasional tokes on yesterday's joint bloomed up in a sea of bohemian atmosphere. Its meditative strata undulating just above the wood stove. Spontaneous waves and sudden curls hinted at clandestine visits from obscure spirits.

"Yeahaaa. . . . So,so,so . . . la ti do. . ." he said rolling up his sleeves. "Spent last summer collecting driftwood . . . among other things. The sea. . . . It's alive you know."

Ivan adjusted his headband magnifier and became quiet for a long pause.

Then, in the detached voice of a Delphic oracle, he said, "Found art is nature's art, let intuition guide your splatter-vision."

"Curious notion," I thought.

I was listening, but I couldn't help being distracted by the emergent awareness of a strange motion at the periphery of my vision. An old electric fan wobbled about in a space behind the stove, its humming head slowly sweeping back and forth like a blues singer lamenting a deep tragedy. Its colorful paint of psychedelic abstractions overlaid a background of dull black. I wanted to ask where he got it, but I didn't want to break his concentration.

Ivan became increasingly intense, carefully withdrawing each piece at random. One by one, he handled the driftwood gently as if each piece were a newborn baby. Slowly, he placed them along the floor in deliberate patterns like the pieces of some foreign puzzle.

"Listen . . . just tune it in . . . they've been there . . ." he said.

Ivan kept sorting. Stopping occasionally, he carefully inspected the swirls and grains that logged the ancient voyages of conniving roots and adventurous branches. Then he handed me a certain specimen. A streamline crow with no feet, smoothed out by countless currents and moody storms from ages long gone by.

"That's a rare one," he said.

The grain of the wood mapped out the feathers and eyes and beak. I thought it strange so much detail, yet just a natural piece of driftwood. It seemed to have a silly grinning expression. I couldn't imagine where it fits in the growing puzzle across the floor. I just put it back in the basket.

The throbbing warble of the antique fan began to hum a slow melody, its rhythm morphing in a muffled mantra: "Thrum, thrum, thrum. . ."

"What an imagination," I thought.

Then he warble became increasingly clear, almost as if it were trying to say something: "You, you, you. . ."

Across the floor, its sweeping breath fluttered the pages of unfinished poems and stray sketches of wilderness scenes.

Suddenly, the fan emitted a definite chant: "Who are we, who are we, who are we?"

"Ivan! Did you hear that!?" I asked, nodding toward the fan.

Then a distant voice spoke: " ... Driftwood sails the Sea of Dreams, 'till it finds the shores of consciousness ... But you have to find your own. ... Comes with the wind, goes with the rain... "

I just looked at him. His glazed eyes staring out through the infinite flow of modal reality. A breeze curled his beard ... I took a toke ... then reached in.

Next morning at the kitchen table, I studied the map trying to decide the best route back. Woman poured a coffee as sun beams drifted across the clay pitcher. I wished I could stay longer. So far, I'd gotten only obscure allusions to what I knew was an arcane question. For some reason, if Ivan knew, he couldn't tell me. At least not directly.

Then a cloud of gun solvent wafted in as Ivan entered the kitchen. He stopped by the wood stove and withdrew something from the ashes. I prayed he wouldn't ignite; I put down the map.

"Ivan, which way should I go back?" I said.

Ivan sat down at the table, carefully turning the chard twig over and over as if reading an ancient scroll.

"Being a free spirit is the only meaning life can have," he said, grooming down his graying beard.

Then he began staring at something across the table.

"Now there's a fine example of a free spirit!" he said.

Ivan began sketching on the back of a napkin. I leaned toward the work. A portrait of a little lizard resting on his six gun began to emerge.

"Nevada," I thought. "Nevada . . . I've never been to Nevada."

Ivan rode me back through the woods in his old dune buggy. Boarding my truck, I could see that trickster grin growing across his face. I knew something was up.

"You are your own path. You'll know it when it happens," he said in that gravelly voice of his pioneer persona.

Douglas firs bowed a farewell as winds whispered in code. It began to rain as I drove away.

CHAPTER 8
THE PATH

Morning's clarity filled the sky as I departed the Reno Motel. Looking over the map, the road to Ely seemed to promise a nice scenic drive. Nevada! All new country to me. A holiday ride to remember.

Miles of road wandered along through mountains of chaparral and plains of desolation. Mirages appeared and disappeared in a magical performance of morphing dunes. Mile after mile, ephemeral ponds, ethereal roads, and floating lakes appeared then vanished. They came from nowhere. They returned to nowhere.

It was a lonely road, yet beautiful in the sincerity of its simplicity. But an unsettled feeling began to grow as realized I had seen no sign of civilization for several hours. Somewhat spooked, I glanced at the map.

"According to the map, this road definitely came from someplace, and it defiantly goes someplace," I said with hesitant reassurance.

Still, an aura of isolation hovered above. Just then, a windsock emerged out from a mirage. Then a wooden gate, then a hazy hanger wobbled up from a curve in the road.

"Hey, looks like an airport over there. Must have missed the sign," I thought.

It was 3 p.m., and I needed a break, and besides, I felt that special airport urge.

CHAPTER 9
THE ATMAN CRUX

The dusty road wound around to the airport entrance. A gate was open. I stopped and pondered the aloofness hanging in the air. The place seemed so deserted except for a laid-back guard dog. As I stepped out the truck, the black dog seemed duty bound to bringing me a well used shop rag laying it at my feet. He insisted I pick it up. A well mannered dog, I thought he might be part Labrador.

"Good boy," I said. "Good boy. . ."

I looked for a name . . . no collar. Then he shuffled back to his main station on the mat beside the Quonset hut, occasionally looking back to make sure I was following along. Passing through the gate, I looked up and ahead.

"Hey! A DC3, just look at that! What a classic airplane," I said to myself, walking across the ramp. "Tan, green, and gray, looks like an Army Air Corp C47. Wonder what it's doing here?"

All those rivets, all that workmanship, all that history. A real veteran. I looked on with amazement. Her head held high against the blue sky. Two big radial engines proudly stood out from the glorious wings of adventure. Her beautiful figure posed with pride in the sunny spotlight of the airport ramp, cargo door slightly cracked open.

"This bird must be at least fifty years old. Beautiful as ever. Wonder what all she's been through?" I said to myself. "Odd ... no tail numbers."

Walking all around, I noticed strange flora protruded out from the wing tip navigation lights. Oil streaks coated vintage dust under the wings. Bug guts painted the leading edges. And a vague aroma of herbs wandered through the atmosphere.

"What's she been up to anyway?" I wondered.

As I walked back toward the office, I noticed the door propped open. An old radial cylinder head stood at attention like a doorman waiting to usher me in.

"Hey!" I said. "Anybody home?"

No one at the desk. Dusty maps and virgin logs lay scattered along a glass counter hazed over with the scratches of countless transactions. Cans of motor oil and flight plotters occupied the bottom shelf. Concrete slab peeked up through peeling linoleum. I sure was glad to see an easy chair in the corner; I needed an easy rest. Then I noticed piercing springs extruding out from the seat. I felt an inspiration for another walk.

"Who all sits there?" I wondered.

The faint scent of avgas wafted in through the wandering trails of airport air. No one around. No posters. No signs.

"What airfield is this?" I wondered. "Perhaps the management's gone to lunch."

Stepping farther along the walkway, I could see crows playing in the thermals rising up from the warm runway. Echoes of distant chirps bounced around the spacious emptiness of the maintenance hangar. Huge doors of steel clicked and squeaked in the light winds stirring up from the lonely landscape. The walk along the ramp was a welcome change from riding the truck most of the day. My tired eyes drifted down from the clear sky to find a sun cured bench overlooking the runway.

As I sat down, I laid out dog's chewed up shop rag next to me. Maybe the wind and sun would dry it out. It reminded of the time Dozer brought Ivan that old chewed up veil, or whatever it was.

"See through the veil," Ivan would say.

Just for fun, I picked up the old rag and tried to see through it. Ahead of the bench stood a simple granite memorial. It was for veterans of some foreign war. I began reading the inscriptions.

"All those names, ranks, and dates. What does it all mean now? All those lives, who were they, and for what?" I asked myself.

The polished memorial and all its secrets sat nested in its own shadow cast by afternoon's sun. It reminded me of a question Ivan had raised back at Toli Creek:

"Is life a reflection of a shadow or a shadow of a reflection?" he had asked.

Seated there on the antique bench, I couldn't help thinking something was anomalous about this trip.

"Why did I get the jitters when I first picked up the recorder? And just what did Ivan mean by saying 'You'll know it when it happens'? Until what happens? Perhaps it's a metaphor describing the exhausted summation of life's end. Or maybe it's the vision-quest of a phantom soul fabricated by the machinery of mind," I thought.

I had come all this way to ask the most spiritual man I knew the meaning of "self," but his answer was always a Delphic allusion to something unnamable. Maybe I would never know. Or maybe it was a thing beyond explanation.

But I had always wanted to know. In the afternoon of life, I wondered what it would it take to actually apprehend this thing that was its own subjective experience of being, and discover why it was such a mystery.

The congenial solitude of the small, laid-back airport was a welcome interlude in the long journey home. It had a simplicity and sincerity that invoked feelings of being totally at ease. Its quietness, its openness, its invitation to the spiritual freedom of soaring ideas. Even the crows seem to appreciate the ascent of its sacred currents. The airport was the nexus between heaven and earth. The airport was my secret temple.

More drowsy than fully awake, I slipped off my shoes and got comfortable on the weathered bench. The granite memorial reminded me how short is life. I couldn't help but wonder if this trip had been a failure.

Half asleep, I looked out at the runway, mindlessly watching the rising curtains of heat waves rippling up in hypnotic undulations. Hanger doors clicked and bonged with the periodic rhythm of a ghostly beat. Bird chirps echoed on through a timeless afternoon.

A breeze fluffed my hair as exhausted ambition began to yield to the weary doubts of life's impossible dreams. Shimmering twinkles closed my eyes as I submerged in the warm sea of sunbeam's aura. I took a deep breath. It was utterly quiet.

Just then, Crow landed on the memorial and said, "In this world there is a puzzle. You can have the prize inside if you can open it."

For some reason, I got a creepy feeling he was hiding something too eerie to think about. And now my aversion to thinking about it was provoking an unsettling feeling that something was amiss. It was a feeling like witnessing the contradictions in a master magician's best act. They seem so real, yet so impossible. Only now it was me, my own self that was the object of the impossible act.

"But surely I'm a real self, conscious of what I know to be real. Or am I? Maybe I shouldn't think about this," I said to myself.

"How to open the puzzle?" I wondered.

Crow was still standing on the memorial. I was about to ask, but his eyes said the answer must come from within. As I looked down in meditative puzzlement, my eyes drifted along the memorial surface. It was a strange feeling when I suddenly realized all the names, all the ranks, all the dates, these had all vanished. Nothing. All that remained was a polished blank stone.

Looking in, I realized I could see myself as if I were inside the stone. My reflection had been there all along, I just hadn't noticed it. I had been distracted by the names, ranks, and dates of all those lives gone by. I had the odd feeling that I'd been in this place before.

Looking on past my own reflection, it dawned on me that I was simultaneously outside the stone looking in and yet inside the stone looking out. It was if I were living in a symmetrical world of reflected reality.

"Which is which?" I thought. "Well, it doesn't matter because this is silly."

Then a small cubic niche appeared on the memorial surface. The cube began to grow and grow as it sunk down into the stone, gradually expanding until it formed a vacuous cube within. Then the cube merged into the center, filling the totality of my own head.

"What a strange illusion," I thought. " ... 'Illusion' … Right?"

"Wait a minute ... Is that me or is this me?" I said with increasing alarm.

Just to be safe, I reached up to my head for reassurance.

"NO!! What's happening?" I said, "My head ... it can't be a cube!"

Then the cube spoke: "So who are you?"

"What do you mean?" I said.

"Are you sure you want to know?" it replied.

Startled I said, "What are you, why are you in my head?"

No answer.

"Who is this?" I demanded with growing dread.

"Whoever you want it to be," said a voice of a nonchalant traveler.

Somehow, someone or something had hacked into my mind. It was a feeling of supreme humiliation.

"This is my mind, and now I'm being evicted by an invisible stranger? Get out!" I said. "This is crazy."

"Who am I?" it asked.

Somewhat taken back by this question from nowhere, I said, "This is me, dammit, and I mean to get in."

"But do you really want in? For that would be to forsake your name, your rank, your dates. Are you sure?" it said. "Are you really sure that you're sure?"

"Okay," I said to myself. "I have here a material body, but somehow my essence is caught in limbo. I have to find it."

I insisted on being myself even in defiance of an invasive phantom that had just now demonstrated the power to hijack my mind. I was horrified to consider the possible retaliations. Who knows what it might do to me?

Freezing fear shot up my veins. I knew I was in over my head.

"Maybe it's better to just leave this thing alone. Maybe I can still back out," I thought.

"No, dummy, death is preferable," I said to myself. "I've come too far. The entity is upon me right now. What can I do? I have to capture my essence and do it now! But how?"

My heart pounded the panicked pace of a presto beat. Eyes squinted the fearless gaze of a red alert. Ears swept back to combat mode. Something in me had just decided to fight.

"Being a free spirit is the only meaning a life can have," I thought.

Suddenly, I felt a grip inside my head. It was trying to collapse my skull! I tried to pull back, but it was too powerful.

"What if I lose my mind? What horrible fate awaits?" I thought. "God! What is this?"

I rubbed my hands together until I felt a tingle bloom. Moved by unseen forces, my hands rose up then crashed down upon on my head.

I began to pray: "Orpheus, if I must go to Hades to find my soul then so be it."

The vacuous cube that filled my head began to tumble and undulate with ambiguous waves. I was astonished to witness this cube as it turned itself completely inside out! Then my mind turned itself completely outside in! The memorial began to wave; it was waving to me.

"Who is this?" said a voice of optimistic faith.

"Whoever you want it to be," I said with the voice of a defiant pioneer.

I took a breath of exasperation and said to myself, "Indeed. Who am I really?"

Then the phantom said, "I am the perpetual presence at the moment of creation, and it's been that way all along."

"Who knows who we really are?" we said in unison.

I awoke in a temporary state of amnesia. When I opened my eyes, Crow was still standing on the monument.

He said, " ... Comes with the wind, goes with the rain ... "

Then he turned and took off into the wind. Wings thrashing at full throttle, he ascended up through layer after layer of dissipating mist, ripping open veils of pious subjugation. I held out my hands to catch the raining shards of fragmentary memories. I was uninjured, but confounded. The fragments were incredible.

Awestruck, I said, "Can this possibly be?"

I felt like I had been totally disconnected from all that was familiar and was just now standing on a ledge overlooking a whole new world. I questioned everything.

"What just happened?" I asked.

"This is me." I said.

I rested my head in my hands.

"I can't believe this," I said.

"Whoa! Man! Watch it!" I said, clutching the wheel. "Must have dozed off for a second. Better stop someplace for a rest. But where am I now?"

I checked the compass and glanced at the map.

"East bound route 50, gassed up at Sparks around 10 a.m., now it's 3p.m. Let's see, that would put me ... ?" I tried to figure.

Whoosh! Slam! Errrrk!

"Turn to the skid, NOW!" I shouted, near panic. "Wow. What was that? Stray gust almost blew me off the road."

Then a flurry of snow whizzed through the cab, rocking me side to side. Getting the truck back under control, I thought it odd.

"Snow on a clear day? Must be a freak weather cell of some kind," I said to myself.

I continued east for a few miles, and then I began to feel it: A psychic residue lingering in the cab. Somewhat alarmed, I looked around. It was as if someone had just been sitting there!

"What is this?" I said. "Must be fatigued to the point of being delusional. I'm going to have to rest, and soon. Someplace."

Then a sign post just up ahead: "Eureka".

Hotel Ruby's road sign promised: "Telephones in Every Room." A bed would do me just fine. It was a clapboard building with tall arched windows and steps of stone worn to a dip. Sparks tingled my fingers as I reached for the brass doorknob. Tiles lined the vestibule floor. The steam radiator clicked and knocked, its paint peeling like the bark of a hickory tree. The faint scent of cigar smoke reminded me of a curio shop back in Boma.

Afternoon's sunlight poured in through tall windows of wavy glass with little bubbles illuminating an antique lobby. Its carpet cut for a different floor plan. Black and white TV played to empty seats of secondhand furniture. Walking across the lobby, I noticed a dusky room of drawn shades. It seemed the adjacent dining room had been frozen in a different era. The dusty cord across its entrance promised, "Open Soon After Maintenance."

Behind the main desk, a grandfather clock guarded the wandering rips of ancient wallpaper. Its faithful tick tocks invoked a mood of fatalistic mortality. Roman numerals and the slow pace of a brass pendulum said I would only get so many tick tocks per life.

I had to ring the desk bell three times before the clerk emerged from the back office. Bugs littered the globe lamp hanging down from the high ceiling. Chirps of parakeets echoed out from somewhere in the back. Then an old man, mostly bald with wire-rim glasses, opened the guest book. He seemed formal and proper, his suit in style fifty years ago. His face logged the saga of life's hardships, but a humble optimism shone through. His hands trembled as he handed me the key.

The room had a telephone like the road sign promised. A dial-up phone.

"Maybe I should call Ivan," I thought.

I picked up the receiver. No dial tone. It was quiet, very quiet. Its disconnected wires lay draped behind a small desk. Their entangled ends lay in waiting like shoelaces lost with nowhere to go. The bed smelled like disinfectant spray. I was utterly exhausted.

I kicked off my shoes and reclined on a worn out mattress. In a daze, I stared at a ceiling of wrinkled plaster. Each wrinkle casting its own bad-lands shadow, slowly growing in the creeping rays of a retired afternoon. In a forlorn room in the back of an antique hotel stationed somewhere on the outskirts of Eureka, Nevada, USA, planet Earth, I tried to sleep. For some reason, I kept thinking about Murdo.

Strange dreams of shadowy beings and chaotic detours through fantastic castles appeared throughout the night. Black curtains with important business cruised along corridors of granite. I would suddenly awake with an explosion in my head, then fall asleep dreaming I was out of my body. I was dreaming I was awake, a red sphere flying beside me. Being weightless in the truck came back in flashes. I could smell gasoline. Somehow it involved a crow. But then

I realized I was no longer dreaming. Unnerving memories flooded in like the surge wave just before a storm. I couldn't sleep.

"This is incredible. These memories . . . they can't be true, can they?" I thought. "Maybe it's just how I look at it."

CHAPTER 10
CRITIQUE OF THE INCREDIBLE

Predawn, I left Eureka talking to myself: "There's got to be a logical explanation. How can I understand this? In a few hours I'll be in Salina, Utah. Another four days, and I can be home in time for work."

Two days later, I was approaching North Platte on Route 80. All this driving, and all I could think about was the absurdity of what seemed to be a chaotic array of impossible images. It reminded me of Ivan's surreal paintings.

"Something really strange must have happened at Murdo ... What?" I said out loud.

Just ahead, a "Route 83" sign post appeared. I checked the map.

"That's the road north to Murdo. Maybe I should go back to Murdo," I thought. "There's got be an answer somewhere. But then I would be a days late for work back in Boma."

I got a queasy feeling even thinking about returning to Murdo. I was afraid of something.

"I am my own path," I said to myself.

The drive north to Murdo became increasingly unnerving. I was having to fight my own irrational aversion to an imaginary danger. It seemed an absurd problem, but the fear was real, the struggle fatiguing. I was becoming exhausted. I turned on the radio, hoping some country music would help keep me awake. I heard buzzes and static and a few distant stations. It reminded me of Ivan's old radio back in Ohio. Then came a clear station from somewhere across the plains.

"Lord ! ... Don't move that mountain . . . just give me the strength to climb . . ." wailed out the close harmony of gospel singers, The Hoppers.

After a stay at a road-side motel, I arrived at Murdo early in the afternoon. Just like before. It felt like I was heading to court to stand trial for some grievous crime punishable by death. I forced myself to stop at the same gas station and then on to the car-show museum.

"All these artifacts, so familiar, yet they're all foreign. There's that '57 Chevy. I always wanted one like that. But who's the mannequin behind the wheel?" I wondered, " ... He wasn't there before ... Maybe I'm just another kind of mannequin."

I made myself drive up and down the same street, looking for a clue, a hint, or anything that could make sense of the incredible memories of just a week before. Then I came to that same cafe at the end of town. I stopped.

"I don't want to do this!" I thought. "I've got to do it."

The sight of its door made me nervous. I forced myself to enter. Seated at the same table, I ordered coffee just like before, though I really didn't want it. There were a lot of customers. They looked to be both locals and transients. I was familiar with their species, yet they all looked like foreign animals.

"Just look at those strange ears sticking out," I thought. "And the new waitress, she has ten fingers."

In the busy atmosphere, I discreetly looked down at my own hands in amazement. Ten fingers. It was as if I had never seen them before. Everyone was chatting about something.

"Whatever are these creatures talking about?" I wondered. "What do they think is important?"

Exiting the cafe, I retraced the same exact steps across the parking lot, carefully turning over suspicious looking stones as I went.

"Surely there's an answer here somewhere," I said looking all around. "Nothing, nothing. Maybe I should head out to that same rest stop just west of town. Maybe it's in there."

It was late in the afternoon when I pulled up to the rest stop. My heart was quick. Nausea pressed my stomach. I forced myself out the truck and looked all around – only prairie and fences all the way to the horizon.

"See ... no monsters," I said to myself with faux confidence.

Just then I remembered their command: "Don't look at the red one."

Immediately, I aimed the monocular at the forbidden spot. Nothing. But an eerie feeling came over me. In a kind of psychic perception, I sensed an invisible wall right behind me like someone's hands hovering right behind my ears. I turned about to face it. It radiated a texture of familiarity.

"This is the same wall as in my dreams," I said. "It's right here, just waiting. Hey! This is the clue!"

My hands reached forward as if to touch something.

"I have to try, I have to overcome this," I said, pushing forward.

Suddenly, something yanked me through.

"Oh! God, what is this?" I yelled out.

"Don't be silly stupid, you just tripped," I said catching my balance.

I kicked away the little stick entangled between my shoe laces.

"This is just a rest stop. This is just an ordinary rest stop!" I said out loud.

Out of curiosity, I reached down and picked up the guilty stick. Slowly, I stood up. Unblinking eyes scanned the horizon for something too subtle to see.

"Or maybe it's not so ordinary," I said to myself. "This stick ... it's that same piece of drift wood Ivan handed me back in Oregon. The one like a smoothed-out crow ... I thought I put it back."

I put on a jacket and sat on the hood. I turned the little crow over and over just wondering how it got here. He still had that same silly grin.

"Hey, amigo, what's there to grin about?" I said."Who knows, maybe aliens need a rest stop too."

As evening turned to night, I laid back on the hood and looked up at the stars.

"The sky. . . It's alive you know," I said to Little Crow.

My watch read twelve o' clock midnight exactly. It was the instant between yesterday and tomorrow. Then I surprised myself with a spontaneous utterance:

"I am the perpetual presence at the moment of creation, and it's been that way all along. Who knows who we really are?" I said.

"Yeah. That sounds familiar," I said to myself.

I put Little Crow in my shirt pocket.

Along the road to Ohio, I called the boss to let him know I'd be late for work. All the way back, contradictions struggled for coherency. Possible and impossible. Emerging memories of alien beings clashed with trusted models of reality. I knew it was true, but I couldn't believe it.

"How can memories of the incredible be reconciled with the conventional world view? Must have been a dream," I said. "But the time laps through Murdo, that's objectively knowable, and it's objectively inconsistent."

Three days later, Ol 'Man LaRue's grain elevator appeared on the horizon. He used to give away free peanuts to us kids. Across the fence, spring leaves were just budding in Sonny Hudson's apple orchard. I'm home, I thought, maybe. Then the Boma water tower appeared and reassured me reality was still intact. A crow buzzed my truck. A suspicion haunted my mind.

CHAPTER 11
THE UNPACKING

Afternoon sunbeams painted a portrait of the old rooming house I'd been calling home. Mrs. Franklin was in the kitchen fixing a salad.

"You're a little late getting back, aren't you, Willard? I suppose it involved some woman, didn't it?" she said, slicing up a cucumber.

"Pretty good," I said, snatching another piece.

In the next few days, I was back fueling airplanes, mowing grass, and brewing coffee.

"You've been awfully quiet since you got back, Willie," Earl said as he poured himself another coffee. "So how'd it go?"

After so many lessons, I had become quite attuned to my flight instructor's tone of voice. He was genuinely concerned.

"I'll tell you when I figure it out," I said.

Skyler, the airport dog, whipped my legs with enthusiastic greeting. He never asks embarrassing questions. He just sits around on his mat, waiting for airplanes to come in. And then jumps up and tries to round them up like so much cattle. I feared for his safety, but somehow he always out-maneuvered danger. I thought the was part border collie.

Some weeks later, I had stopped to gas up the old truck. I'd been working late that night. It was very dark. Suddenly, an alarm went off!

"That smell of gasoline ... " I thought. "There's something dangerous nearby!"

For a moment it scared me. Memories of a dark road flashed through my mind. But that feeling evaporated as I drove on home. Later that night, scary dreams of shadowy beings roaming along through granite channels filled my mind. I awoke with a memory of being extricated from my body. A strange being was asking me to play a harp. Back at work, memories of a red sphere would suddenly appear right on the runway.

As an assimilated man, I felt compelled to doubt the reality of an experience profoundly deviant from conventional world view. But these memories were too vivid and too persistent to simply dismiss.

Twice, I had the same dream.

A shadow man speaking in a kind of psychic feedback loop said, "Don't scare the musician, this is his first experience with an alien."

Then later, the same one said, "Who are you really?"

I began taking notes.

Being so far from home, I had kept a strict account of time, fuel, mileage, and money.

"It seems thirty-three hours went missing," I said to myself as I studied the trip log."But no extra fuel or mileage or money were expended. This is really curious."

All summer, the scary dreams continued. Their content became more specific and coherent. I kept taking notes. Just as I was becoming comfortable with my shadow friends, the dreams were no more.

I stopped at a payphone to call Rapid City FSDO, Flight Standards District Office, to ask if they had any reports of an "incident" or any radar anomaly in that area at that time. They had no such reports. The man asked "why". I hung up. For a month, I ran an ad in *The Coyote*, Murdo's local newspaper, seeking any witness to an "incident" in that area at that time. No reply at all. I called the weather station in Pierre asking about any unusual weather phenomenon near Murdo last February or March. I didn't know if reports of normalcy were good or bad.

"There's no maps beyond the frontier," as Ivan would say.

It was my day off. All morning I sat on the floor of my small second floor room. For a while, I just stared at the clouds drifting the sky beyond the window. Then I pulled over the basket of stray notes. I picked up Little Crow, turning him over and over, wondering.

"I have here a basket of bizarre notes. Now how does this fit together?" I said to myself, "This is too incredible to ask anyone for advice. I'll have to get off the grid and assemble this one myself."

"Maybe some classical music might help," I thought as I turned on the shortwave.

By accident, I tuned the radio between stations.

"That static ... it's so familiar. It's like the sound of rain," I said to Little Crow. "It's totally spontaneous. Hey, that's the voice of creativity."

I set Little Crow on the floor beside the basket. Slowly, I began laying out the notes across the floor like some foreign puzzle. I sorted the notes by their apparent temporal order. I sorted them by their level of objectivity and apparent certainty and level of internal consistency. A form was taking shape.

I researched what was known about unusual phenomena in the earth and in the sky. I researched the history of Murdo. I researched the psychology of delusion. I tried to weigh all this against the probability of an alien visitor as estimated by the shepherds of conventional science.

"I have a dilemma," I said to myself, "but a new reality won't be coming with any instructions."

The next morning, I sat out on the porch inhaling autumn's inspiration.

"I'm gone for a walk, Mrs. Franklin," I said, stepping out toward town.

Standing on the bridge over Sundog River, I found the water high and hurried. Pine trees waved like family at a train station. Then, a faint voice at the edge of perception just barely came in through the river's noisy rush. It was like a distant station struggling through static. I began to tune it in as my psychic antenna abandoned the known world.

". . . Is that you? . . . Is that you? . . . Is that you?" asked the raspy voice of the old river.

Overt waves and covert currents informed a narrative of River's perpetual creation. Curtains of rain swept peaks of froth across the flow of eternal change. Secret wars erupted between established rocks and renegade branches. The chaos of conflicting whirlpools resolved in smooth currents later downstream only to be stirred up again by yet another bend. Then the sky became clear. I reached into my pocket.

"Comes with the wind, goes with the rain," I said to Little Crow.

CHAPTER 12
THE MUSE OF PRACTICAL REASONING

It was late afternoon back at the rooming house; I poured me a glass of whisky. Quietly rocking in the back-porch glider, periodic glints of sunbeam envoys refracted their way through the elixir of communion. Their vital message slowly seeping in, one swing at a time. Back and forth, the rhythm of revolution was in no hurry.

"Helios! . . . Here's to you," I said, sipping the sparkles of atomic inspiration.

I pulled Little Crow from my shirt pocket. Gently rolling the drift wood over and over as if it were a living being. I had to wonder where he came from, what all he'd been through.

"Hey, Little Crow, it seems we're both on a journey of some kind," I said.

I had set out to Oregon to ask Ivan the meaning of "self" as if it had an objective meaning. His response was always an evasive maneuver.

He would conjure up my presence through tricks, and stunts, and provocations of surreal discourse. Then back off, leaving me alone to witness for myself the struggling emergence of the authentic self.

And then there was Murdo. Murdo visitors seemed to have the same idea, but their tricks a little more radical than attic door surrealism.

I began to wonder, "Is Ivan somehow related to the Murdo visitors? They seem to be kindred spirits. Would either of them have told me? Should I even ask?"

By seeking, I had become a self that seeks itself that seeks itself . . . ad infinitum. I was the manifest nonsense of an infinite regress to the objective world from without. But from within, I was the subjective experience of being something indefinable and autonomous. So many of my genus have insisted on the objective meaning of their essence even in the face of conflicted insight. I'd been one of them.

"Maybe there really is a rift in the species," I thought. "Ivan's non-answer makes perfect sense."

"Creativity doesn't come with instructions," he would say. "It's always a surprise if you can find yourself."

"I think I'm beginning to understand what has happened," I said to myself as I sat up in the glider. "It's the Seeking! ... By seeking, I've become an independent essence."

Pine trees whistled and cheered with impromptu gusts.

"Independence overthrows the supremacy of orthodoxy and liberates the principle of creativity. 'Seeking' is a transformative act. A rite of sorts," I thought. "But transforming, ... transforming ... into what . . . ?"

In the dread of an liminal state of being, I realized I'd just stepped off the conventional world, and into the unknowable nucleus of authenticity itself.

"This must be the same fate for all who seek themselves," I said with increasing alarm. "By seeking . . . I've become one of THEM. . . . So, what happened to ME ? What should I do now?"

Little Crow just grinned and said, "That's for you to answer. Just be yourself."

Whoa!!. . . What!! . . . I lurched back in shock. Stunned by the radical transformation of the mundane, I stared in awe at the transcendent entity in my hand. I didn't know what to say. After a long pause of spiritual recalibration, I took a hearty pull. The world just became a more mysterious island. Another swig. I could hear the drumbeats . . . A different reality began to sink in.

"So, so, so, amigo. . . .Welcome to Earth. . . . I'll bet you're on a mission," I said. Then I had to think: " 'Be yourself'? What does that really mean? Let's see . . . myself is what seeks itself. I am the indefinable conclusion of an infinite regress. My reality is subjective. My authenticity my own. My intentions independent."

"But that's descriptive, not prescriptive" I thought.

The neighbor's cat crept under the picket fence. He knew he wasn't supposed to be there. Mrs. Franklin had often tried to run him off for chasing her birds. Crouched down in the tall grass, he watched intensely the backyard bird bath.

"Now there's a fine example of an independent spirit," I thought. "He won't be changing his ways for anyone; they have been honed for millions of years."

I looked out at the distant clans of conspiring pines convening in important meetings.

"But how can being independent possibly prescribe what I should do?" I wondered.

Little Crow said, "Being an independent spirit is being the strategy that can never be invaded. It's the same for all who seek it. And now that's you because you asked. It's been that way all along."

Across the yard, apple trees were beginning to bear. I thought it beautiful. Ivan once said my own aesthetic is half the reality.

"Well, that's because my aesthetics co-evolved with apple trees," I thought. "And a stalking cat co-evolved with small game."

"Me? . . . an un-invadable strategy ?" I wondered. "How is that prescriptive?"

Little Crow rose up in my hand. He looked all around the world, then he turned and looked me in the eye.

"We've always been the conscious agency of adapting worlds," he said. "You can't beat that." Just then cat looked up at Crow.

"Cat has his calling. . . ." said Little Crow.

Back in the house, I set Little Crow in his nest beside my window. I'd made it from moss and bark and stolen twigs. It approximated what I'd seen in the woods. That evening, I sat alone in the parlor, staring in the gas fireplace. Something was coming together.

". . . What a project . . ." I said to myself.

Next day, I jogged over to Boma Street Cafe. The doorbell jingled. Jerome was sitting there next to the big window just sipping coffee, minding his own business. I was breathless as he looked up. I didn't know if I should ever tell anybody.

"But how to do this?" I wondered.

He could see in my eyes something serious was on my mind.

The End

.